TAMING THE BEAST

SEDONA VENEZ

WANT FREE SEDONA VENEZ BOOKS?

Sign up for Sedona Venez's Newsletter and receive FREE BOOKS. In addition to the free stories, you will also get special pricing, exclusive previews and news of new releases.

GET A FREE SEDONA VENEZ BOOK!

Join Sedona's mailing list to be the first to know of new releases, free books, special prices and other author giveaways.

https://sedonavenez.com/free-book

HOPE

I WAS STARK NAKED—AGAIN. With huge ebony breasts swaying, ass jiggling, and designer stiletto-encased feet slapping against the dewy grass, I sauntered over to the center of the clearing.

Perching myself on top of the smooth boulder—or what I now lovingly called my rock of shame*—I surveyed my recurring fixation.*

My heart seemed to freeze and then pound. "Damn. You're such a beautiful kitty," I whispered.

Water cascaded off the tiger's magnificent reddish-rusty coat with narrow dark-brown stripes as he prowled out of the river toward me with rippling muscles. Its chest, throat, muzzle, and the insides of its limbs were creamy with a milky-colored area above the eyes that spread onto his cheeks.

When I extended my hand, he tilted his large head down, rubbing against it with a chuff-chuff *sound.*

"Hello, my big kitty. I'm happy to see you again, too," I answered his greeting. My digits trailed up to the white spot present on the back of its ear.

He nudged my hand away before circling me, his fur caressing my bare legs while I admired the prominent ruff on his head and long tail ringed with noticeable dark bands.

Warmth radiated throughout my body as his fur deliciously tickled me.

"Every dream, you bring me here to watch you swim, and I still don't know why."

My mouth fell open when a deer pranced up to the river and drank from it, completely oblivious to the tiger's presence.

The tiger stilled, waited, and then pounced. The deer didn't even have a chance to run away before the tiger's big-as-saucers paws latched on to its hindquarters, bringing down the deer. The tiger gripped its neck, delivering a crushing bite to its prey. The deer stopped thrashing.

My fingers touched my parted lips before I closed them. "Holy shit."

This was a new addition to my nightly dreams. He'd never killed game before.

Wasting no time, the tiger dragged its dinner toward me, laying the carcass at my feet like an offering.

I gave him a weak half smile, trying desperately not to hurl at the sight of the dead deer. "Thank you, kitty, but it's a little . . . rare for me."

He flicked his tail, making a chuff-chuff *sound, before his limbs quivered, shifted, and morphed into a very naked tall, muscular human.*

"Elijah?" I stammered.

This couldn't be right. Animals didn't transform into humans, especially not into a man I was crushing on hard in real life.

"Yes, my Hope," he uttered in a dark, masculine voice.

Electricity sparked in my body as my eyes perused his mouthwatering splendor. His short, thick black hair had hints of gold, and his beard was well groomed. But it was his stunning but strange amber eyes with gold flecks that always made my stomach flip-flop, like a fish out of water. His eyes were the windows to his soul. They bored into me with an intensity that made my sex clench.

"Damn. Even in my dream . . . you're fucking splendid," I declared. My eyes trailed down his hard body to his engorged, perfect shaft standing at attention.

He clutched my face between his enormous, calloused hands. "Eyes up here, darling." His face dissolved into a exquisite grin. "Unless you're finally ready to get on all fours for your big kitty?" His hands dropped away and grabbed me around the waist, yanking me against his naked body.

"My, you're such a dirty pussycat, and I love it." I licked his bottom lip.

"So that's a yes." It was a statement, not a question.

"Baby, I'll do whatever you want . . . however you want. But only if you promise to lick all my cream, like a good kitty."

We stared at each other with my legs straddling one of his rock-solid thighs.

"There's nothing good about me, darling, but I can promise to lick you to the very last drop." His voice was thick with emotion. "Just say when, my beautiful mate."

Forcing one droopy eye open, I raised my head from the pillow and then put it back down. Rolling over onto the other side of the bed, I flipped over onto my stomach. Pressing my face into the pillow, I screamed, "Shit, that was the best fucking dream . . . ever!"

The cleft between my legs was still convulsing from the memory and magnificence of Elijah Beastie—aka Beastie.

Damn. Elijah is my walking vibrator.

No other man had ever made me feel so utterly consumed, possessed, and ready to throw myself at his feet, professing my undying devotion. And I wasn't even a love-at-first-sight woman. I was more like a fuck-at-first-sight chick.

But with Elijah, it was different.

From the first day I'd met him, there was an instant connection, a spark that tethered me to him. And for a whole damn year, almost every night, I'd been crawling into bed with Elijah's name on my lips and my fingers playing with the moist, warm folds between my thighs.

It was embarrassing and problematic because wanting a man

who was within my reach that I couldn't have was fucking with my head. Big time.

I rolled onto my back, staring at the ceiling. Of course, there was a really easy solution to my dilemma—say yes to his offer to take me out on a date and see if it led anywhere.

Problem solved.

Not.

My relationship with Elijah was complicated. He had made it all too clear he was interested in seeking and destroying my ass in every sexual position possible. My fists clenched. *No.* There was no way I could take him up on his offer. Carter's money and power reached far and wide, and the walls of the mental hospital wouldn't stop my stalker ex-boyfriend from trying to kill Elijah.

I already had one person's blood on my hands. I would be damned if I risked another.

❧ 2 ❧

HOPE

Shit. I'm late. Harper is going to kill me.

And as if she had a GPS on my ass, my cell rang.

Hitting the button on my car's control panel, I answered, "Yes?"

"Where are you?" Harper requested in a singsong voice.

"Don't start. I slept in. My flight getting in from L.A. last night was delayed." I was exhausted from flying in from Los Angeles after choreographing a routine for my celebrity client who was scheduled to perform at an awards show. "Just grab a table, and I'll meet you at Redemption."

She groaned. "I'm not there yet. I just got off another conference call with Knox."

I laughed. "How's my favorite badass rock star, Knox Gunner, doing?"

"He's blissfully happy with his girlfriend, Storm Credence, but somehow still finds time to micromanage me via phone." She breathed out. "I swear, if he asks another damn question about if I have everything handled for tonight's charity event, I'll choke him to death. He acts like planning and hosting a full-blown affair was on my Top Ten Things to Do in Life. Not even fucking close. But I can't say no to the pain-in-the-ass rock star."

"Pain the ass? Oh, please, you adore the man. You probably have several *I Love Knox Gunner* T-shirts stashed in your closet." I chuckled because Harper loved to play the tortured servant when, in fact, she enjoyed working for Knox as his well-paid personal manager.

"Don't get sassy, Hope Pippa," Harper drawled. "My nerves are already frayed from being thrown into the deep end of this event-planning thing." She snorted. "I thought music superstars were divas, but they don't compare to the drama of dealing with a celeb chef who doesn't seem to understand the meaning of light-menu affair." She paused. "And speaking of divas, how's my former client?"

I tapped my fingers against the steering wheel, waiting for the light to turn green. "She's pissed and dumbfounded about my decision to retire from working as her personal choreographer."

I'd deliberated for months before pulling the trigger and deciding to walk away from an empire built on my blood, sweat, and tears. I'd been dancing professionally for seven years, starting out as a backup dancer for a pop music superstar to catapulting myself into the spotlight, building an impressive résumé by being featured in numerous television shows and music videos, along with choreographing world tours, live performances, and awards shows.

I'd traveled to places that most people had never heard of and rubbed elbows with eccentric celebrities who crowned me the new *It* girl. It was an ego boost, proving to naysayers within the dance world that I was a force to be reckoned with, despite the fact that they thought my hips were too wide, my ass was too big, and I would be perfect if I just lost forty pounds.

I pulled off with the changing of the light. "She offered me an obscene amount of money to stay on, but I turned it down. My heart and soul are just not into dancing anymore. It's become what I feared most—just a job." I zipped in and out of the snarl of Manhattan traffic. "Lately, I've been feeling like there's something more than just going through the motions of life. I just need time to think. To evaluate. To explore."

"You're turning twenty-five in a couple days. Birthdays always make people wonder what's next. Plus, you've been working nonstop for years without taking time just for you. You're fucking stressed, drained, and exhausted, and we both know you haven't been fucked in at least two years. The latter would be enough to make any woman crazy."

"Sex is the last thing I need right now," I replied dryly.

"Correction—it's the first thing you need. And I know just the man who can make you all better. Your Eli—"

I cut in. "Don't say it."

"Your Elijah," Harper chanted.

"He is not mine. I'm not the girl for Elijah. I come with a whole lot of baggage and a psycho ex-boyfriend to boot." Every time I thought about my ex, Carter, I could feel an anxious knot tightening in my stomach, making me feel like I was suffocating.

"Why do you have to make life so difficult? A gorgeous, intelligent, caring man thinks you're hot, sexy, and downright amazing, and you turn that shit into some fucking reality show. Give him a chance. You two would be so good and happy together. There's a genuine connection, real chemistry."

My nostrils flared. "Not happening. I wouldn't wish Carter's insanity on my worst enemy."

"How many times do I have to tell you Elijah can handle any bullshit Carter might bring his way? And don't say you don't want to talk about him, because we are going to. I hate that fucker Carter, and I've never even met him. I despise him for emotionally scarring you so badly that you're scared to let Elijah into your life, to love again with no restraints, no hesitation, with no worry of him trying to ruin your romantic—" She broke off her scolding. "Shit. That's my brother calling—again. The jackass is consumed with culling tonight's guest list like some drill sergeant."

I was happy to switch from the subject of Elijah. So I latched onto her momentary distraction. Twitch, Harper's overprotective older brother, was a topic that always seemed to send her into a ranting frenzy.

"What did you think would happen when Twitch found out you were taking over the planning and hosting of Ryker's kinky charity affair?" I remarked.

From what Harper had explained, Ryker Alfero was Knox's brother, and whenever Ryker threw a get-together, it would become the hottest invite in the elite, rich social circles. He'd only invite his affluent associates who were more than willing to give generously to his charitable foundation, all for the privilege of taking part in events notoriously known for its overindulgence in freaky, sensual exploits. Each event was bigger and more scandalous than the one before.

"First, tonight's event is not kinky. It's sexually titillating," Harper pointed out.

"Oh, tomato, tomahto," I taunted. "You can wrap it up in all the pretty words you want. It's still a kinky freak show for rich asshole men to get their rocks off while tossing crisp hundred-dollar bills at gyrating eye-candy."

"First off, I'll have you know, I classed up tonight's event," Harper added. "And second, I don't need Twitch getting all big brother on me. He just shoved his ass into the planning and told me he was handling security. He started grumbling something about making sure the fucking vamps stayed out and threatened to throw them out into the sun."

My eyebrows squished together. "Vamps? Sun? What the fuck does that mean?"

"What?" She coughed. "Oh, nothing. You know him. He says crazy shit like that all the time. I swear, his job is making him turn into a suspicious weirdo."

"Uh-huh," I responded. "And what exactly does Twitch do for a living?"

When I asked about her brother, she ignored my question, but I was too exhausted to probe further. Besides, I knew from experience it wouldn't net me any information. For some strange reason, Harper was secretive about what her brother did for a living, and all she would tell me was he worked in law enforcement. Doing what, I had no clue. Every time I'd tried to get more info, Harper clammed up. And for a woman who had no qualms about telling me what flavor lube she'd used with her latest conquest, the secrecy was bizarre.

Harper's voice interrupted my thoughts, "And talking about crazy, I need a favor. A girl dropped out of the dance-off tonight, and I need you to take her place."

"What?" I sputtered. "Hard pass on that shit. I'm not shaking my moneymaker onstage."

"But it's for the children," she whined.

"Then I'll write you a big, fat check," I countered.

"What's the fun in that?"

"I'm not doing it, Harper. Why don't you fill in for the missing dancer? You can dance . . . kind of." I snickered.

"I'm a blond bombshell with no fucking rhythm. The most I can do is whip my hair around and hope to holy hell I don't trip over my fucking feet. Plus, remember the twerking incident?"

I broke out laughing so hard my stomach started hurting.

"Don't laugh," Harper protested.

"I can't help it."

It had been a hopeless endeavor when I tried to teach Harper how to twerk for a sexy Valentine's routine she'd insisted on surprising her then-girlfriend with.

"All you had to do was put your ass into the move," I teased. "Damn, you were a hot mess. You have no rhythm at all."

"Fine, make fun of me. I might have been lacking in the dance department, but I was right on beat when I got her in bed." She laughed.

"Too much information. I don't need the visual." I scrunched up my nose. "And the answer to your request to dance is hell no," I snapped.

"Hope Pippa, stop being an ass. You owe me one." I could hear the exasperation in her voice.

"Come on, Harper. I don't feel like getting all dressed up to parade around like some peacock. I just want to spend tonight curled up on my couch in yoga pants, binge-watching my favorite paranormal shows." It had been weeks since I'd been home, and I just wanted to veg out to paranormal hunters searching for Bigfoot and the Swamp Man.

Harper scoffed. "For the life of me, I don't know why you waste your time watching that paranormal garbage. Swamp creatures and Bigfoot don't exist."

"Whatever. Moving on . . ." I laughed because it was a long-running joke between us.

Harper was in the Paranormal Shit Is So Fake camp, and I was in the Paranormal Shit Is Based on Fact camp.

As the niece of a professor of archaeology, I was fascinated by the strange and unknown. I had grown up listening to my uncle's tales of traveling to exotic places for digs and seeing all the strange fossils he'd unearthed over the years. It'd planted a seed of obsession with ancient cultures and creatures in my head.

"So, as I was saying, I'm busy tonight. I have a hot date with my remote."

"Hope, you're doing it," Harper stated. "Just be prepared to wear something sleazy."

"Are you out of your damn mind? I'm not—"

"I've got to go. See you in a few. Bye."

When our call ended, I turned up my music to distract me from going snap, crackle, pop. "I'm literally going to strangle her with her own hair."

The Manhattan traffic was congested, so it took me longer than anticipated to arrive. I relinquished my car to Redemption's overeager valet before taking a few quick steps toward the inconspicuous doorman, who opened the door, allowing me to step into the dim upscale restaurant. I was trying to hide my excitement and morbid curiosity. This was my first time being at the well-known private restaurant owned by a former model named Vivica.

With a long waiting list, Redemption was more of a VIP restaurant patronized by the rich and famous. It was also known that Vivica would scrutinize each guest. But the difference between this restaurant and other frequented celeb hotspots was everyone who came here wanted their privacy because of the type of acts that would take place here at night. Sexual acts would be orchestrated on a stage for all to see while patrons ate, watched, and—given proper motivation—had their own private shows in their secluded booths.

It didn't take long for me to be greeted by stares as I hurried along. At almost six feet tall with rich ebony skin and blue eyes, I stood out. According to social media friends, I had curves in all the right places with a figure designed for the catwalk, which had earned me a coveted spot on the Top Black Female Choreographers and Dancers You Should Know list. As a size ten, with what my social network followers called *flawless curves*, I was one of the rare dancers who also had breasts that were real, albeit large.

A willowy redhead with ample cleavage on display approached me with a huge smile. "Welcome to Redemption. I'm Vivica, owner of this sinful establishment." She gestured dramatically.

I observed the celebs inconspicuously sauntering around.

I smiled back. "Thank you. I'm meeting Harper Ducaine."

"I just seated her," she gushed with a sultry voice. "Right this way, darling."

She looped her arm through mine as if we were best friends. Surprisingly, I didn't mind. Working in the entertainment industry for years had fine-tuned my fake and creepy people radar, and Vivica didn't put out any of those vibes.

I admired the expensively designed restaurant draped with rich fabric across the ceiling. The Moroccan flair made the space feel both exotic and elegant. The whole middle section of the floor was wide open, making way for the strange circle configuration of several booths with high backs and wide sides that faced toward a large platform, which pretty much obstructed the chance of any voyeurs.

Vivica practically glided across the floor. "You're Franklyn Bishop's niece," she stated, matter-of-fact.

I shot her an incredulous stare. My uncle and I didn't look anything alike. We didn't even have the same last name. "Yes. How did you know?"

"Birds of a feather flock together. It's a small world for people like your uncle and me. So I make sure to find out everything about people worth knowing." She winked at me. "And you, darling, are one of those individuals." She arched a well-manicured brow.

I had no clue what she was talking about. "And exactly in what capacity do you know Frank?"

"Eons ago, he was one of my favorite clients when I was a Credence O. escort."

I almost stumbled.

Wait, what? Did she just say escort?

There was a fluttery feeling in my belly.

"Are you sure we're talking about the same man? Franklyn Bishop, professor of archaeology?"

"Of course I'm sure." Vivica chuckled. "The stories I could tell you about your wild uncle." Her eyes twinkled. "I guess he didn't tell you about that, huh?"

"No . . . he didn't. My uncle's sex life is not a topic I ever want to know or talk about." I tipped my head to the side.

Plus, it was really hard for me to believe Frank was even interested in sex. He was too consumed with archaeological digs and unearthing the next big ancient ruin.

"But those were the good old days." Vivica exhaled noisily. "It's unfortunate about his recent troubles."

I knitted my brows. "What troubles?"

She waved a hand at a guest, totally ignoring my question.

I decided to try again. "Vivica—" A flush of adrenaline tingled through my body.

"And here we are," Vivica announced.

She stopped before a table occupied by not only Harper and Twitch, but also the man who made my stomach pop and gurgle like a freshly opened bottle of Pellegrino—Elijah Beastie, aka Beastie. My hands moistened and my eyes locked onto Elijah, who was appraising me with smoldering amber eyes.

Damn.

He looked good enough to eat in his crisp white shirt open at the collarbone, displaying his golden skin covered with intricate tattoos.

Redemption's booth wasn't made for huge men like Twitch and Elijah, who were built like they belonged on a football team. But somehow they'd managed to cram themselves on opposite ends of the booth with Harper in the center.

"Here she is, Elijah." Vivica gently nudged me forward. She gave him an amused stare. "So you can stop scowling like someone stole your bike." She winked at me again. "Have fun, darling. This tiger's a keeper," she drawled before sauntering away.

Elijah stood patiently. "You're late," he informed me with a velvet voice. "I thought something happened to you," he added while placing a warm hand at the small of my back, ushering me into the booth.

While sliding against the seat, I considered him from head to toe and back again to his hard lips. They looked like they rarely smiled, which completed the don't-fuck-with-me aura.

"Well, hello to you, too," I replied before leveling Harper with an irritated stare. "I didn't know you and Twitch were joining us." I kissed her cheek.

Harper gave me a hug before responding with an exaggerated, "Surprise!" and jazz hands.

Twitch waved at me. "Hey, baby girl." He grinned, as he

leisurely studied me. "I'm here to give Harper the benefit of my infinite wisdom, as big bros tend to do."

I rolled my eyes. "Turn down the crazy a notch."

Twitch was the exact opposite of Harper. She was a tall, curvy platinum blonde with a year-round natural golden tan. With jet-black hair cropped in a buzz cut, Twitch was a tightly muscled, massive man who looked like he could bench-press a car. He was intimidating until he smiled, flashing a dimple.

He upped the wattage of his smile. "You know me . . . I was born crazy."

I gasped when Elijah's lips grazed the shell of my ear. "Is there a problem with me being here?" he asked, his voice dripping with raw sex. He took my hand, clasping it tight when a jolt of electricity ran through both of us. His thumb caressed my digits.

My clit thumped against my panties as an erotic image flashed through my mind—me on all fours and those big hands all over my body while he fucked me from behind.

A soft growl left his lips when my tongue snaked out to wet my lips.

Shit! Shit! Shit! I'm in serious trouble.

Crossing my legs, I replied, "Not at all," with more calm than I actually felt.

Staring pointedly at our clasped hands, he squeezed hard before releasing mine.

I added, "It's just a . . . surprise." *Like an unexpected run-in with an ex-boyfriend when you didn't take the time to put on makeup and were looking a hot mess.*

Shit, if I'd known the object of my lust—whose image I would use to get off during many hot and sweaty nights of masturbation—would be here, sitting next to me, with his hard thigh pressed against mine, I would have sexed it up a tad.

Damn. This isn't good. How the hell am I going to get through lunch?

It'd been a year since Harper introduced me to Elijah at one of her notoriously outrageous parties, and he still treated me like no other man I'd met before—with respect and care—despite the fact that I'd pushed him in the only-friends category when he clearly wanted more. But Elijah hadn't gotten all aggressive and pushy like most men would have in that situation. In fact, he'd done quite the opposite. He'd backed off completely.

Now our interactions were far and few between. It was like he was deliberately trying to avoid me, which frankly irked me.

"Here," Harper snapped, shoving her tablet into Twitch's hand. "This is the updated guest list." She took a sip of water, accusingly staring at him. "I could have emailed it to you instead of you inviting yourself to lunch."

Twitch pulled a lock of Harper's hair, and she promptly swatted him away.

"How else would I be able to see my baby sister, who refuses to make time for her big brother?" he asked.

Harper tapped her lip with fake seriousness. "Like everyone else—by setting up an appointment with my pimp, Knox Gunner."

"Smartass," Twitch growled menacingly. "It's not nice to joke with an alpha, you brat."

Ladened with dishes, the waiter and another server approached the table. "Beef tenderloin skewers with chimichurri salsa, truffle mac and cheese, and Parmesan truffle fries," the waiter announced as the server grandly set the small sharing plates down in the center of the table. "And two medium-rare steaks." He set one plate in front of Elijah and the other before Twitch. "Enjoy," he finished with a bow of his head.

Elijah smiled, a slow lifting of perfect lips, to reveal straight white teeth. "We took the liberty of ordering."

"I see," I croaked before clearing my throat.

The waiter beamed at me. "What would you like to drink?"

"She'll have a Grey Goose and tonic," Elijah answered.

Damn. The man even knows my favorite cocktail.

He continued. "And I'll have a Jack on the rocks."

"Make that two," Twitch added.

"I'll have a gin and Dubonnet," Harper chimed in.

The waiter and server roamed away.

Twitch flicked his finger across Harper's tablet, reading the guest list. His head suddenly snapped up, eyeing Harper. "Oskar Orlov? Absolutely not," he barked. "He's not coming tonight. He's a—"

"Quiet, you big oaf." Harper popped him on the hand—hard. "We have company." She scooted closer to him, whispering something in his ear.

I could feel the heat of Elijah's stare. His physical magnetism was palpable. I calmed my breathing as I glanced over at him. He turned toward me, patiently watching me.

Shit, no man should exude so much sex appeal.

His black hair with hints of gold kissed his collar. His well-groomed rich black beard added a hint of roughness to his lean, hard face. His white shirt outlined his hard muscles. Elijah was dark, deadly, and absolutely delicious. He was also trouble.

But right now, all I could think about was how beautiful he would be stretched out across my bed, completely nude, with me running my tongue over every inch of his tan skin.

My body pulsed with need. I could resist my attraction to him for only so long. Years of denial without sex was coming back to bite me on the ass . . . hard. Now my defenses were down, and I was salivating over him like he was a cupcake with lots of yummy frosting.

Elijah took a long sip of water, glancing at me over the rim of his glass. "So, Harper—Troublemaker Number One tells me you're dancing tonight."

I raised a brow. "And I guess that makes me Troublemaker Number Two?"

"Yes, but you're the best type of trouble, the kind I'd love to get myself into . . . every fucking night," he replied huskily.

My womanly center squeezed hard, as if he'd yanked it with his invisible pussy-magnet power.

"That sounds . . . real promising, but I'm the type of bad girl you don't want to bring home to mama." I bit my bottom lip.

"I wouldn't worry about that. My mother would love you."

I cleared my throat. This was the rabbit hole I hadn't wanted to go down with Elijah. From nervousness, a bead of sweat trickled between my breasts.

Sweet baby Jesus, I'm sweating like a glass of lemonade on a hot July day.

We eyed each other for a full minute before I couldn't stand the silence anymore. "So, to answer your question, yes, I'm dancing tonight. If you're coming, be prepared to break out the crisp hundred-dollar bills."

I brought the glass of water to my lips, sipping slowly. The small diamond tiger pendant hanging off the silver bracelet on my wrist tapped softly against the glass.

His amber eyes sparkled with pure seduction as his calloused finger caressed my wrist, causing my entire body to clench. "I'm happy you wore the bracelet I got you."

I swallowed hard over the lump of emotions.

When Harper had dropped off the bracelet, a recent gift from Elijah, it was totally unexpected, since I'd never even discussed my birthday with him. But it was shit like that—him taking the time to learn things about me—that would bring a smile to my face.

My fingers ached with the need to touch him. "Thank you. It's beautiful." I glanced away and then back. "You didn't have to get me anything for my birthday. Besides, my birthday isn't for another couple days."

"I wanted to get you something that would remind you of me." His lips curled up into a small smile.

My body craved to be touched by him, and as if he sensed my need, he suddenly leaned in, putting his nose against my neck. My lips parted as his alluring aromatic scent of expensive cigars, sandalwood, and rich earth wafted around me. I almost dropped my glass before carefully placing it on the table with trembling fingers.

He leaned away, and when he pulled a small plate over in front of me, his arm brushed the side of my breast.

Scooping a teeny portion of truffle mac and cheese onto a plate, he dug into it and held out a forkful. "Here, open up for me, darling."

Butterflies fluttered in my stomach. "You do know I'm not a two-year-old?" I countered.

But there was something sexy about him feeding me, and it aroused my senses and body.

"Open your mouth, Hope," he demanded in a voice that was low, seductive.

My breath quickened. *Well . . . if you insist.*

My lips parted, allowing him to slide the fork inside. *Damn, it is good—in every fucking way possible.*

He pulled the fork away, intently watching me. My nerve endings stirred as I chewed slowly.

I cleared my throat when I noticed Harper with her chin propped in her hand, ogling us with rapt attention. The damn woman was enjoying seeing Elijah seduce me. From the glint of smugness in her smile, I knew she was planning a fantasy wedding with Elijah and me in great detail. Elijah's erotic play and me lapping it up only confirmed her belief that he and I were made to be with each other. And she was right—but under way different circumstances.

He cut into his steak and ate a forkful of meat while staring at me. He swallowed before saying, "I've been meaning to talk to you."

"About?" My throat was parched. Picking up my glass, I drank thirstily.

"Us," he purred. "We've known each other for a year. But we don't really know each other. I want to fix that. Just you and me in an intimate face-to-face. All you have to do is say the time and the place."

I fingered my bracelet. "You mean a date?" My breathing accelerated.

"Of course," he retorted.

I bit my bottom lip, remaining silent. My stomach churned with fear—but not from Elijah. It was from being so close to giving in to temptation. I swallowed down the thick longing, forcing myself to think before I did something I would regret, like throwing caution to the wind. Deep down inside, I knew I was already addicted to Elijah in a most troubling way.

Contrary to common sense, I slanted my body in his direction, grazing against his broad chest. "Elijah, that's not a good idea." I was surprised at the huskiness in my voice.

He arched down, rubbing his nose against the sensitive spot on my neck. "Why?" he mumbled.

Pushing him back slightly, I answered, "Because it would be messy and complicated, and I don't do messy and complicated."

"This is not difficult, Hope. I want to get to know you better." His lips pressed together.

"Not doable." But my body wanted to do this. This pull between Elijah and me was primal.

What I wouldn't give not to care about the ripple effects of giving in to him.

But, of course, my mind rebelled.

"I'm pretty sure it is, darling." He moved closer, erasing the distance between us.

Before I knew what was happening, he swooped down, his tongue darting out to intimately caress my neck. Then he nipped my neck so hard that jolts of pleasure shot straight down to the slit between my legs.

I inclined away. "What's with the touching? I don't like to be touched," I croaked, praying he wouldn't pick up on my lie.

He watched me with delicious intensity, which immediately made me all hot and jittery again, before he softly fisted my hair with one hand, bringing my face mere inches from his.

"Really? Because it looks and feels like you love my touch," he responded with a sensual swirl in his voice. His fingers started to comb through my hair.

I didn't even bother to move. I relaxed into his grip. I was uncomfortable that he saw me too clearly. It was frightening how my body reacted with one glance from him, one inflection in his voice. What was infuriating was that he was right. I loved his touch. I loved it way too much, and that was the fucking problem.

I licked my lips as I examined his brooding golden appearance, and all I could think about was how badly I wanted to sit on his face and ride him like a stallion.

No, no, no. This is a fucking mistake.

I knew deep in my gut it would never be as simple as sex with Elijah. Frankly, I would be disappointed if it was.

"Elijah, I . . ." I didn't even realize I was slowly moving toward his lips until my cell rang. "Sorry. Just let me see who it is." Pulling out my cell from my handbag, I immediately recognized the number. "Excuse me. I have to take this." Flicking my finger across my phone, I answered with, "Hold on for a second."

Elijah growled with displeasure before scooting out, allowing me to get up from the table.

I quickly walked out of the restaurant and to the entrance, stepping into the cool air. "Cassidy?"

"Hello, Hope."

"What's going on, Detective?"

"I don't have good news for you. Carter was released," he commented bluntly.

My heart pounded against my chest. "How? Why?" My mind was a jumbled mess as my thoughts ran a mile a minute.

One breakup, seven months of Carter stalking me, three world tours, an order of protection, an innocent man killed, and me left nearly dead after being stabbed by him—and now Carter was out?

I should have seen all the red flags from the moment I met him. I should never have gotten involved with him.

His voice was tight when he related, "I don't know how he got released from the mental hospital early. But you'd better believe I'll find out."

I knew Detective Cassidy would. I trusted him. Of the members of law enforcement I'd dealt with during my harrowing incident with Carter, he was one of the few who'd actually looked at me like more than just another annoying case they had to deal with. Cassidy actually cared and had been keeping in contact with me over the years, checking in with me every so often.

"How long has he been out?" I rasped while fingering my handbag, feeling the weight of the 9mm I'd been carrying around for years.

"According to my sources, it's been two weeks."

"He's going to come after me again." My fingers trembled around the cell. "You know that, right? And he'll try to kill me again."

My life had changed dramatically after Carter—my crazy, psycho, obsessive stalker ex—brought destruction and mayhem into my life.

The fucked-up part was we hadn't even had one of those crazy-in-love relationships. He wasn't even my type, which was ruggedly sexy and funny. Carter was the opposite—cocky, spoiled, and a trust fund baby.

But there was something about Carter that I'd found strangely appealing, an attraction I still couldn't unravel until this day. And after two months of dating, the fairy-tale romance had all come crashing down when I discovered he had another girlfriend—a socialite who fit perfectly into his world —and I'd ended the relationship. But what I hadn't realized was he was mentally unstable—a fact that had come to light when I started receiving numerous bizarre text messages and phone calls from Carter, telling me he couldn't live without me and to give him a second chance. I'd started documenting everything, and then I'd filed police reports. He'd been arrested and charged with stalking. And I was granted a lifetime protection order.

That was when shit had taken a dramatic turn.

Months after Carter and I had broken up, I'd gone on a date with another man. Carter had shown up, brandishing a knife, and stabbed my date for fucking with his property—me. Then he'd turned the knife on me before a waiter tackled him.

Only I survived, and after months of therapy, I'd thought that part of my life was over and I was free from him. But I'd received a hard lesson about the many benefits of being rich—one being a get-out-of-jail-free card. Carter had avoided jail by claiming he suffered from schizophrenia and entered into an agreement to seek help in a luxury mental health ward.

"But, this time, when he tries to kill you, you'll stop that fucker in his tracks," Cassidy corrected with deadly calm.

Off the record, Cassidy had recommended I take self-defensive classes and get a weapon to protect myself, and I'd taken him seriously.

I surveyed the congested Manhattan sidewalks. "I'm a fighter. You know this."

"You be careful, Hope. You have my number. Call me anytime, day or night."

"Thanks, Cassidy."

After our call ended, I walked back into the restaurant, feeling emotionally deflated.

Elijah quickly stood, allowing me back into the booth.

Harper quirked a brow.

I mouthed, *Later*, to her.

Then I grabbed my Grey Goose and tonic, thirstily gulping it down. The liquid smoothly slid down with a slow burn before hitting my belly.

Elijah sharply regarded me. "Is everything all right?" he probed.

"Yep. Everything is fucking peachy."

I slammed my glass onto the table with way more force than

I'd intended. It tipped over, and I attempted to clean it up with my napkin, frantically dabbing at it, when Elijah covered my trembling digits with his big, warm hand, stilling my agitated movements.

"Hope, leave it," he whispered.

I yanked my hand away and watched the vein along his jaw pulse. It was the only telltale sign of how annoyed he was by my reaction.

I glanced over at Harper. "I'm sorry. I've got to go. Call me later, okay?" I added before considering Elijah. "It was great seeing you, Elijah."

"As always, it was a pleasure, darling." He slowly kissed my fingers before sliding out of the booth.

Finally standing up, I started to walk away when Elijah grabbed my elbow with one hand and texted with the other.

My cell beeped.

"That's the text I just sent you with my phone number. Call me anytime."

I didn't even bother to ask how he'd gotten my cell number. I glared at Harper and then walked away.

❧ 3 ❦

ELIJAH

HOPE WAS A VISUAL STUNNER. When she'd strutted into Redemption with her fierce confidence, bold taste, and toned figure, I'd stared.

How could I not?

Hope exuded a hip-thrusting sensuality that would intimidate most men, but I wasn't like most men. I was a tiger-shifter determined to claim my mate—Hope.

She was luminous with her perfect smile and smooth ebony skin. Her skintight black dress had slid over her curves like it had been designed solely for her. Its hemline stopped several inches above her knees, allowing me a glimpse of skin. She'd been part smolder and part fury when she walked over to the table. A curvy six feet, she'd made my fingers clench. I unabashedly craved her.

From the moment she'd sat down, I'd fought to keep my mind off her intoxicating scent, but the honey-sweet aroma of her wet sex had filled the air like perfume. My tiger had rattled his cage, fighting to get out. My hands had fisted as I tried to contain my inner beast with all my might. Hope was the one I'd been waiting for all my life. My tiger had known the second I met her.

She was mine. My mate.

But Hope wasn't ready for me. I could tell by the way she tried to stamp down her own arousal. She wasn't willing to give me what I needed—her trust, her heart, and her body. I could feel her distress from fighting her needs and emotions. I just couldn't figure out why.

I glanced at Harper in the rearview mirror as she muttered into her cell, "Hope, slow down. You know I can't understand you when you get all worked up like this." She remained silent and then cried, "What? Oh my fucking God. How?" After pausing a beat, she exclaimed, "Detective Cassidy?"

I peered over at Twitch. We knew Shawn Cassidy, NYPD detective, from our dealings with law enforcement on small cases involving humans. And if Cassidy was calling Hope, there must be some serious shit going down.

"I, uh—shit, this is bad." Harper fumbled with her leather handbag. "No, I'm not home yet. Twitch and Elijah are driving me there." She paused with a sheepish expression on her face. "Of course not, Hope. I'll call you as soon as they drop me off."

I pulled up to her brownstone, and Harper barely waited for my vehicle to stop before flying out.

"Thanks," she mumbled without even looking back.

"Fuck no," I barked, jumping out and slamming the door behind me. If something was going on with Hope, I wanted to fucking know what it was.

Taking my cue, Twitch was out of the car in a flash, grabbing Harper's elbow.

Her eyes widened as she snatched her arm away. "And where the hell are you two going?"

"I have to use your bathroom," Twitch responded.

"What?" She suspiciously looked at him. "No. Go home," she hissed before turning on her heels and rushing away.

Twitch and I were fast and in close pursuit.

"Nope. I've got to go, sis," Twitch drawled.

"What are you? A two-year-old?" she grumbled, pushing her key into the lock.

We deliberately crowded her, knowing, given the opportunity, she would slam the door in our faces the minute she stepped into her brownstone.

She frowned at us over her shoulder. "Okay, Shifter One and Shifter Two, step the hell back. You're breathing down my damn neck like I owe you money."

I crossed my arms. "Stop stalling, Harper, and open the fucking door," I demanded.

She whirled around with her blond hair flying. "Watch the tone, Elijah Beastie." She glowered, poking me hard on the chest. "I'm not one of your shifter targets." She huffed before turning back around and stepping inside.

We shoved past her before she even had time to turn on the lights.

Out of habit, I sniffed the air for smells of intruders—shifters, vampires, or humans. Then I scanned the house, watching for signs of disturbance, but saw none. Twitch nodded at me before escaping toward the back of the house.

We had worked together for years on dangerous Rogue missions, so I knew the routine. Twitch was doing a security sweep of the house while I prepared to corner Harper for information. She wouldn't stand a chance against our interrogation techniques.

Harper tiredly plopped down onto her sofa while I stormed into the kitchen, opening her refrigerator and grabbing a bottle of water.

"Yes, go ahead. Take a bottle of water, Elijah Beastie," she snapped. "So rude. Don't even ask permission," she quipped.

I gulped the water, lifting my shoulders in a half shrug. "Don't need permission. We're family."

Harper was more like a sister to me. Even though it was rare for tiger- and wolf-shifters to get along, Twitch and I did. We'd formed an unlikely kinship when we started working for Rogue as Others Hunters. Twitch's family had quickly become mine, and that included Harper—the annoying baby sister who tagged along, trying to be one of the boys. I knew her well, and she knew me just as well.

She rolled her eyes, tapping her cell against her palm. "What's taking Twitch so long?"

Twitch stormed into the room, giving me a slight nod. Everything was clear with no signs of a break-in or intruders.

Harper hopped to her feet and marched over to the door. "Well, okay . . . bye, you two." She snapped her fingers. "I'll see you tonight at the party." She yanked open the door with a jerky movement and then gestured dramatically for us to get the hell out.

My eyes bored into her before I calmly headed over to the door and slammed it shut with a thud.

She rubbed the back of her neck. "You two have to go. I really don't care where. Just get the fuck out. I need to make a private call."

I gently nudged her toward the sofa.

She slapped my hands away. "Don't you manhandle me, Elijah." She glared at Twitch. "And why are you sitting down? That's the opposite of leaving."

Twitch crossed his beefy arms. "Sit down, Harper Elizabeth Ducaine," he ordered.

"Using my middle name? I must be in real trouble," she huffed before plopping down.

"What's going on with Hope?" I asked quickly.

She examined her manicured nails. "None of your business."

Okay, if this is how she wants to play it . . .

I sloughed off my leather jacket and pushed up my sleeves before sitting down on the coffee table directly in front of her, deliberately crowding her. "We're not going anywhere until you tell us what's going on."

"Why are you all up in my face?" Harper complained.

We both gave her our alpha stares. She squirmed uncomfortably.

"I know what you jackasses are doing, and I won't fold. This is a personal matter." She sniffed with disdain. "It's Hope's personal matter, so don't ask me another damn question." She glared at us.

Twitch scooted over into her space, and she shoved him.

"Really?" she snapped.

Twitch studied her. "Hope is like a sister to me, so if there's something wrong, I want to know."

"Whatever." She stubbornly watched him before arching a brow at me. "And why do you care, Elijah?"

My nostrils flared. "Okay, I'm done playing games with you, Harper. You know exactly why I care. Now tell me what the fuck is going on."

From the first moment I'd met Hope a year ago, I knew she was mine, but convincing her of that was proving difficult. Every time I'd pushed forward to pursue and conquer, she'd find a way to evade my attempts. And, as if our relationship weren't complicated enough, she had no clue I was a tiger-shifter.

Harper's bottom lip trembled. "I'm so fucking scared for her right now," she blurted. "Hope has been through a lot of shit, guys." She pointedly stared at me. "And I refuse to see her get hurt . . . again."

Baring my teeth, I barked, "I know you're not suggesting I would play mind games with Hope. You fucking know me better than that, Harper. She's my true mate, and I would do everything and anything within my power to make her happy and keep her safe."

"Mate? It's about fucking time you admitted it aloud." She arched a brow. "You think I didn't figure that shit out months ago? And I'm not implying you would hurt her. I know you wouldn't." She nervously bit her lip.

My inner tiger tensed. "Is she in danger?" I winced as my tiger mercilessly clawed against my insides.

Tears trickled down her cheeks. "Yes. And all I'm going to say on this matter is that her crazy ex-boyfriend is very dangerous, and I'm worried he might hurt her . . . again."

My inner beast roared and pressed against my skin, fighting me to get out. "If you're not going to say how, then you have to get her to stay with you, Harper. She's not safe at her house, alone."

"I'll try, but she's stubborn. You've got to protect her, Elijah. She'll never ask for help, but she fucking needs it. The system fucked her over years ago, and they're doing it again." She grabbed my hand. "You'd be good for her, Elijah. You really care about her, and she likes you more than she'd ever admit. But she'll never tear down her emotional walls and let you in if you try to force it. Just give her some space to figure out what you could bring to the table."

"No." My lips flattened. If I had to camp out in front of her fucking house every damn night, then I would until she acknowledged what we had—the forever type of connection.

"No?" she replied.

"You heard me. No. I've known her for a fucking year, and I've given her enough space to recognize we belong together. I'm done waiting." I ground my teeth. "You either tell me more about what type of trouble she's in, or I'm going over to her house and asking her myself." My muscles quivered from fighting the need to shift, from letting my tiger take control.

"Before we became friends, her ex-boyfriend Carter nearly killed her three years ago, and she just found out he's been released from the mental hospital," she blurted out. "She's been pushing you away because she loves you, and she doesn't want that psycho Carter to kill you. And that's what he's threatened to do to any man she has a relationship with." She pulled her hand away and dashed aside the tears. "I'm her best friend, and if things were different, I know she'd be with you in a heartbeat, but they're not. And I'm telling you now, if you push her, she'll fucking run, and you'll lose her forever."

"Let me deal with that, Harper." My jaw tightened. "I'm done waiting. Tonight, there'll be no doubt in her mind I'm the man she needs."

❦ 4 ❧

HOPE

I PULLED onto Frank's quiet residential block before parking in front of his house. Drumming my fingers against the steering wheel, I didn't know what had possessed me to drive all the way over to Park Slope when I could have just called him. Plus, I didn't even know if he was home. Knowing him, he was probably halfway across the world on some dig. But, right now, I was feeling emotionally raw to the bone. I needed family and his comforting strength mixed with a good, hard cry when I revealed to him Carter was out.

I tried not to linger on the fact that Frank and I didn't always see eye to eye on a lot of things, like his abrupt decision to quit his job as a professor to live a nomadic life in search of archeological treasures. He was still the only family I had left. When my parents had died, they'd left me in his custody, thrusting him into being the caregiver for a newborn baby. As I'd grown older, it dawned on me just how much he'd given up for me, like going on digs. But not once had Frank ever made me feel unloved or unwanted.

Getting out of the car, I eyed the dilapidated door and dying flowers. He had really let my childhood home fall apart. Frank, if nothing else, was a real stickler for order and appearances, but that was before he'd started using his money for more important things, like funding his archaeological digs and, apparently, escorts.

Sprinting up the stairs, I noticed the door was ajar. When I nudged it open, an overpowering scent of rot and decay slammed into me, making my eyes water.

What the fuck is that smell?

It had been months since I'd seen or talked to Frank.

Is he dead?

My heartbeat raced as I rushed into the house, closing the door behind me. Eerily, the space was completely quiet. The worn wooden floor squeaked under my feet as I made my way toward the living room. A prickly cold sensation ran down my spine as I stepped over the threshold and into the living room.

"Please . . . don't kill me," Frank pleaded while being pinned against the wall by a well-dressed tall, brawny blond man.

"What the fuck is going on?" I asked sharply.

My body tensed when the man dropped Frank and turned with a blur of superhuman speed to glower at me. The man smiled coldly, causing the ragged scar that covered the left side of his face to crinkle from the sheer effort. Despite the scar that snaked down from his face and disappeared under his shirt, this rugged man was stunning and had the presence of a person used to getting what he desired. But it was his eyes that were terrifying. They were crimson red and animalistic.

This wasn't a man. He was a monster.

After seeing this frightening monstrosity, a normal woman, which I was not, would have hightailed her ass out of there, screaming for her life—but not me. I stood my ground because this mutant's presence validated my longtime belief in the existence of other beings besides humans on this planet. I just hadn't had any proof of my theory—until now.

Acting out of pure instinct and spiked with a little bit of crazy, I shouted, "Stay away from my uncle!" I pulled my gun out of my handbag and charged toward them.

"Hope, no," Frank croaked.

The monster man glared at me as if I were an escaped patient from an insane asylum, his eyes communicating he wasn't afraid of me.

My common sense completely flew out the window. Feeling absolutely insane and pumped with adrenaline, I aimed the gun at his head. "If you even flinch, I'll shoot."

Frank stepped in front of the man. "No!" he shouted.

I lowered the gun and jabbed my finger at the man. "What is that thing?"

"Thing?" The man peered through the questioning crimson-red pools.

Frank's face turned ashen. "She doesn't mean anything by it." His voice shrilled.

The man's head snapped in Frank's direction. "This is not over," he spit.

I blinked as his deformed face transformed into an unmarred facade, like some sort of magic trick.

What the fuck?

My eyes locked with his, and something simmered behind his cold eyes that chilled me to the bone. The floor rumbled, like we were on the verge of being swallowed by an earthquake, and a putrid smell filled the air.

His eyes were calculating as he loudly sniffed the air. "Why aren't you afraid?" His arrogant, full mouth set in a firm line as he quietly considered me.

"It takes a whole lot to rattle me, and you're not it," I replied coolly. It was the truth. I wasn't the type of woman to panic or get hysterical. It just wasn't in my DNA.

"Interesting," he remarked. He stormed out of the living room before slamming the front door.

I shoved my gun back into my bag, my heart thumping rapidly against my chest. "Like I asked before, what the hell was that thing?"

Frank ran a trembling hand through his thinning black hair.

"Demon," he stated, matter-of-fact, walking away. "I need a drink." He stood in front of the bar in the corner of the room, pouring scotch into a glass with a shaky hand.

Did I mishear him?

My gaze clouded, going distant. "Wait. Did you just say demon?" In quick strides, I was beside him.

He nodded solemnly.

"A demon that possesses people and torments them in hell?" Poking my tongue into my cheek, I waited for his response.

"No, that's all urban legend. Demons are powerful creatures that can morph themselves to appear humanlike, and they kill indiscriminately. But they most certainly don't come from hell."

"But his eyes . . . they looked savage." My voice caught. I remembered the way Carter's eyes had transformed into a crimson-red animal-like gaze while he was cutting into me. I'd convinced myself I'd hallucinated the whole thing, and I'd been having nightmares about it for years.

"Carter is back," I rasped.

"I know," he replied with a wary voice.

My eyes widened. "What?" I jammed my hands on my hips, watching him gulp down the alcohol like water before he poured another glass. "Why didn't you tell me?"

"I was trying to take care of the Carter problem without your involvement."

"What the hell does that mean?" My stomach quivered. "Is he coming for me?"

"I wouldn't worry about Carter. He's the least of our problems now. The Others . . ."

"What Others?"

"Supernatural beings—vampires, shifters, and demons—they're called Others." His bottom lip trembled.

My posture stiffened. "Wait." I held up my hand. "Vampires, as in the Dracula-style undead? And what in the world is a shifter?"

"No. Vampires are not dead. They're just immortal." He

pinched the bridge of his nose with one hand. "Throw out everything you've ever heard about vampires, because it's not true. They're just beings inflicted with a rare blood abnormality in their bloodstream, and it makes them crave human blood. And shifters . . . well, that's a whole different beast—literally. They're beings who are born with inner animals—like wolves, tigers, et cetera—and they can shift into their animal at will."

"Holy shit!" I sucked in a quick breath. "Why don't humans know about them?"

"Do you really think humans are ready to know about the existence of Others?" He walked over to his desk, tiredly slumping into the worn leather chair.

Following him, I sat across from him in a chair. My eyes narrowed on his face. He had bruises under his eyes, and his nose appeared dislocated.

"Frank, what's really going on? What did that demon want?"

His posture tensed. "Hope, I did something really bad." He swallowed hard. "Now I'm indebted to the wrong type of Others . . . demons."

"This is about money? Again?" I gritted out.

Over the years, to fund his digs, he had sold everything he owned and taken out loans from the bank, his 401(k) plan, and even me.

He unbuttoned the top button of his shirt. "The demons gave me a lot of money to find an artifact called the key, a relic I found and decided to hide." His pupils dilated. "I just needed their money to fund my future excavations, so I embezzled some, but I continued to dig for their key. After months of me coming up empty on digs, I thought it would have proven the object didn't exist." He scraped a hand through his hair. "Now they know it does and I've been hiding it."

My chest tightened. "Frank, what is the key?"

"The portal to the demon world has been locked and hidden for centuries." He rubbed his arm. "The key is the only way they can go back to their world."

I threw my hands up in the air. "So just give it to them."

"If only it were that simple." He took another gulp of scotch. "If anything happens to me, I need you to retrieve something from my bank safe deposit box ASAP."

"They're planning on killing you?" A slight chill ran through my body. "Why can't we go to the police? I can talk to Detective Cassidy and—"

"No." He shook his head. "Humans can't get involved in Others' business. It's strictly forbidden and can get you killed." He stumbled over his words.

Leaning forward, I touched his hand, trying to calm him down before he had a stroke. "Okay, just tell me what's in the box. Is it the key?"

He snatched a crumpled piece of paper and a pen from the top of the desk before jotting something on it. "Here's the address for the location of the safe deposit box and the account number." He shoved the paper into my hand.

Nothing about what he was saying rang true. In my head, I was still rationalizing that things like vampires, demons, and shifters lived among us.

"I still don't understand what's going on."

"All the answers will be in the box." He stared into space for a second and then back at me. "Don't ever come back here, Hope. It's not safe."

"Why?"

"The demons know about you now." He stood up and swiftly came around the desk, pulling me to my feet. "I've always been proud and honored to have been chosen as your guardian even though I wasn't your parents' first choice." His eyes watered. "Maybe if they'd had more time, they could have picked someone who wasn't as weak to temptation. And you wouldn't have been in this dangerous predicament I've put you in." His lips trembled. "You're not ready for the chaos to come." He swallowed hard. "You do know I love you dearly, right?" he asked with a strange sadness in his eyes.

I'd never seen Frank look so lost and defeated. It was a scary feeling. "Yes," I replied.

He smiled slightly. "Then that's all that matters. My work is done." Frank pulled me in for a quick hug.

I tightly clutched him before pulling back to stare at him. "I love you."

"I love you, too," he croaked before grabbing my hand.

He led me through the house and stopped before the front door. He gave me one last look. The soreness in my throat and lungs intensified when I noticed the expression on his face. Something about it told me I'd never see him again.

❧ 5 ❧

HOPE

CHECKING out my image in the mirror, I whispered, "Everything is perfect."

But it wasn't. I was a churning pool of dark emotions—fear, anger, confusion, and anxiety.

Demons and vampires were real, and there were beings that could shift into animals.

My mind was spinning from the knowledge I was probably part of a small percentage of humans who knew this secret. Now that the genie—the existence of Others—was out of the bottle, there was no shoving it back.

Leaning against my bathroom vanity, with my fingers trembling, I finished my makeup with a bold red lipstick and eyes decorated in catlike flicks. Then I pulled back to stare at my polished veneer.

I tried not to dwell on the fact that the last thing I felt like doing was attending tonight's charity soiree, but Harper needed me, so I had to be there, front and center. I meticulously picked through my wardrobe, deciding to rock a semi-sheer dress, and since designer shoes were my one indulgence, I donned my favorite pair of silver Coline stilettos, accessorizing with a diamond toe anklet.

Despite my best efforts not to think about it, the image of the demon replayed in my mind. Something deep in my gut told me it wasn't the last time I would see him.

"Dammit." I slammed my palm against the cold granite. I didn't need to add to the insanity that was my life, not with Carter the Lunatic running free.

But maybe he had moved on . . . and was stalking some other unsuspecting woman.

Who am I fooling?

The psycho had made it crystal clear he would never leave me alone. Just remembering how, at two in the morning, he would whisper into the phone, "I love you," and, "Hope, you're so beautiful," still set my teeth on edge. But the ultimate in craziness was his gut-wrenching wail of, "I love you, Hope, and if I can't have you, then no man will," as he'd been dragged out of the coffee shop in handcuffs.

And, as if my life weren't complicated enough, I couldn't get Elijah out of my head, which pissed me the hell off.

My cell started ringing. Harper had called several times, and I'd let every one of them go to voicemail. We hadn't spoken since I came back from Frank's house, but I'd sent her a text, letting her know I was okay. Frankly, I'd just needed some alone time with my thoughts, but I knew her, and she would call until I answered, or in a panic, she'd send Twitch and Elijah over to my house to kick down my door.

I grabbed it. "Hey, Harper. What's up?"

"Don't *hey* me. I've been calling for hours. You can't just go all incommunicado on me when Carter is loose. I'm worried about you," she drawled.

"I sent you a text." I exhaled. "I'm okay. I just needed to clear my mind for a bit, so I drove out to Brooklyn to see Frank."

"And how did that go?" Harper muttered.

I paused. "Interesting . . ."

I decided to take a leap and put it all out there. Harper wouldn't judge; she would listen and accept.

"Do you think it's possible there are beings . . . I mean, people that aren't human living among us?"

There was dead silence, and I thought we'd gotten disconnected, before Harper answered, "Like Bigfoot?"

"No, like vampires, demons, and people who shift into animals, like in the movies."

"Yes, of course," she replied softly. "Why do you ask?"

I had to tell her, or I'd eventually lose my mind under the weight of not sharing. "There was this . . . demon . . ." I slapped my palm against my forehead because saying it aloud made me sound like a raving lunatic. "He had Frank hemmed in, like he was about to whip Frank's ass, when I busted in." I bit my bottom lip before continuing. "Okay, I know how this sounds, Harper—like I'm having a nervous breakdown or hallucinating—but you know I don't bullshit. I'm firmly grounded in reality, but this shit actually happened."

"Calm down, Hope. I believe you."

I sagged against the vanity with relief. "Frank called them—"

"Others," Harper interrupted, "vampires, shifters, and demons, among a few other supernatural beings."

My mouth fell open and then closed. "How in the hell did you know that?" I squealed.

"Hope, I can't talk about this over the phone. It's just that . . . people are always listening to calls, trying to pick up chatter. But I think you should talk to Elijah about your encounter with this demon. He can help you."

"Are you crazy? He'll think I'm insane." I continued. "Can you imagine the look on his face when I say, 'Hey, Elijah, I saw a demon, and it looked like it wanted to eat me—literally. By chance, do you have a demon-slaying knife I can borrow?'"

I laughed with a tinge of hysteria seeping through. "Then, if he doesn't do an about-face from that shit, I'll add, 'Oh, by the way, I'm really attracted to you. In fact, every time I'm around you, I want to get on all fours, push my panties aside, and beg you to fuck me from behind, like a recently released prisoner.

But I'm afraid if I give in to my attraction to you, my stalker ex-boyfriend will find out and kill your ass, tearing your skin off to wear like in *Silence of the Lambs*.'"

Harper exhaled loudly. "When are you going to stop running away from your attraction to Elijah?"

"Don't psychoanalyze me, Harper," I hissed. "The whole point I'm trying to make is he won't believe me." My teeth clenched.

"Oh my fucking God. I don't give a shit if you don't talk to me ever again for saying this, but it has to be said. You are using this whole Carter shit to keep Elijah at arm's length. Yes, there is no doubt Carter is one crazy son of a bitch, but Elijah can and will rip that fucker a new asshole if he so much as breathes on you." She paused. "So here's my humble advice. Get the fuck over it. When you see Elijah tonight, I want you to prance around like the sex kitten you are and tell him you're willing to give him a chance. Then I want you to be open and honest with him."

I'd never heard her so mad. She was right, but I'd be damned if I admitted it right now.

"Is there anything else?" I asked dryly.

"I wasn't finished, Hope," she retorted. "When you're done telling him how much you love him—"

My skin tingled. "I don't—"

"Don't even say it, Hope. Speak the truth and nothing but the fucking truth."

My chin trembled. "Okay, yes, I love him."

"Exactly. Moving on. Now, after you two profess your undying love for each other, I want you to get on your knees and submit. And don't forget to deep-throat his damn big cock like the champion I know you are. That's all. I'm done with this conversation."

I was still silent but allowed myself a small smile at Harper's rant. "Yeah, but—"

"I know. You're dealing with a lot of emotional shit. But you cannot ask him to wait forever."

I didn't respond.

Harper continued, "Unless you're okay with walking away from the best thing that ever fucking happened to you."

"What if it doesn't work?" I had difficulty swallowing.

"It will."

I thought for a second, quiet, considering Harper's advice.

"I've got to go. The staff just walked in, and they need my guidance setting up. But don't think you've been saved by the bell, Hope Pippa. As your best friend, I'm not going to let this drop. If you don't take the leap of faith tonight, you and I are going to have a long talk."

"Didn't we just do that?" I mumbled under my breath.

"Smartass." She laughed. "See you in a few."

When our call ended, I felt emotionally exposed. She was on point with everything she'd said.

After years of swearing I would never let another man close again, Elijah Beastie had snuck in like a thief in the night and stolen something I hadn't known I had to give—my heart.

❧ 6 ❧

HOPE

I STRODE out of my townhouse and down the stairs toward the driver waiting patiently, leaning against a sleek black limo.

He pushed away, tilting his head toward me. "Good evening, Ms. Pippa." He glanced at me from head to toe with an appreciative gleam in his eyes while opening the back door.

"Thank you," I replied, handing him my garment bag and then maneuvering my gown into the limo.

Shutting the door, he scampered around to the trunk to stow my bag before walking over to the driver's side and sliding in.

"My name is Logan," he offered before turning the key and revving the engine.

Pensive, I rubbed the invitation printed on expensive ivory paper. "Hi, Logan," I returned before staring through the window, watching him smoothly drive off into the Manhattan traffic.

My thoughts veered to Harper's advice about Elijah.

Could I really tell him the truth about Carter? And would he still want me if I did?

The car horns of the busy Manhattan streets honked in annoying rhythm. Trying not to fidget in the seat, I peered at the city scene. I crossed my legs as uncertainty crept up on me.

So much about that dark time in my life still filled me with rage and shame. I'd allowed myself to be victimized by a man who refused to accept my rejection. Carter's controlling behavior had left me feeling trapped and isolated. Paranoid that he was lurking in the shadows, waiting to hurt me, I'd locked myself away in my house, only venturing out for work, until I'd had enough and plucked up my courage to get an order of protection against him.

After Carter's attack, I'd vowed I would never let him steal my joy for life. Yet here I was, turning my back on love because I was afraid of the ramifications of Carter's rage.

Well, fuck Carter.

I loved Elijah, and I was determined to pull up my big-girl panties and be truthful with him. If he turned his back on me after I'd revealed my painful past, then he wasn't the man for me.

It didn't take long for Logan to pull up to the gated entry that led to a long circular drive with a private courtyard and fountain. He stopped in front of the entrance to Ryker Alfero's palatial mansion and hopped out, grandly opening the limo's door.

Anxious, I smoothed out the nonexistent wrinkles in my dress before stepping outside. I bit my bottom lip while gawking at the diverse crowd, young and old. Most women were scantily dressed, leaving nothing to the imagination, and men were perfectly polished and refined in formalwear. I could almost smell the money wafting through the air.

I stood on the sidewalk, trying not to fidget, as the impatient pedestrians pushed past me.

Apprehension paralyzed me as I caught my reflection in the glass facade, assessing how the full-length gown featuring a black floral pattern on a sheer backing hugged my curves like a glove. The overlay cleverly covered what I needed concealed but left just enough skin exposed to show I was no angel. The sleeveless bodice pushed up my full breasts. I felt and looked sexy. The dress was daring, seductive, and feminine, and I was ready to dazzle in it.

"I'll drive around back and bring your garment bag inside. Have a good time, Ms. Pippa."

"Thanks, Logan," I stated before swaying away.

The hem swirled around my ankles as my stilettos clicked against the pavement. I approached the man wearing smart business attire and a clear Secret Service earpiece, handing him my invitation.

He glanced down at it. "Welcome, Ms. Pippa. Harper's been looking for you," he announced in a low voice. He nodded toward the two men, who promptly pushed open the doors with flourish.

When I stepped into the grand entrance foyer, the tall ceilings and stone flooring with cherry accents thoroughly impressed me. I weaved through the glittering women and cigar-smoking men sizing each other up, searching for my bestie, who had roped me into joining this circus.

ELIJAH

THE HEAVY POUNDING of the music strummed, annoying me. The charity gala was in full swing, reminding me how much I truly hated these events.

I'd rather take a bullet to the knee than have to socialize with Others. Tigers like me were solitary creatures. We liked to spend most of our time alone, roaming our massive territories, searching for food. Wolf-shifters, like Twitch and Harper, leaned toward pack life and socialization. Both were good friends with Ryker Alfero—alpha of one of the largest and most powerful wolf-shifter packs in New York and leader of the Other Council—and when he called, they would come running, out of respect and friendship.

Ryker was in a hell of a bind since the Shadows had kidnapped his mate, Lightning Credence. Now, all his time was spent trying to locate her—and rightly so, since finding his mate came first. But according to Twitch, Ryker had been stretched thin between his battle to get his mate back and obligations as leader of the Other Council.

I also knew Ryker was between a rock and a hard place. When he'd become head of the Other Council, he'd pledged to unite the wolf-shifters and bring peace to New York. A pledge was the only reason there had been a truce between the Others and his pack. Now that this truce had been broken by a series of shifter and vampire deaths, Others were on the brink of war —again.

Tonight's affair—a charitable event with a freaky, sensual twist for Others who indulged in kinky escapades—was being held to soothe the tension and remind Others that covens, clans, prides, and alphas could coexist in harmony.

Typically, I stayed far away from Others' political bullshit, but tonight was different. Hope would be here, and I was determined to prove to her that she was mine—whether she knew it or not—and that I could protect her as no other human or Other could.

"Man, you're scaring the shit out of the vampires," Twitch accused with a hint of humor in his voice. "They're already a little jumpy from all this shit going down with the Shadows. They don't need a tiger-shifter stomping around like someone pissed in his Wheaties."

"I don't give a shit," I growled. It was the truth. I didn't do well in social situations. I was ornery, temperamental, and had no fucking patience for dealing with Others. I was a top hunter —the leader of an elite special operations team that worked for Rogue—who was more comfortable out in the field, hunting down dangerous Others.

Twitch gave a subtle nod to our security team that blended in the shadows. "Hell, I don't know what you're so grumpy about. This is one of our best assignments. It's a kink event where anything goes." He gestured toward the closed doors that led to different areas where the guests could entertain themselves, all in the name of charity.

I smoothed the sleeves of my tailored dress shirt before running my hand across my hair. "Neither of us is here to play. We're here to make sure none of the guests get out of hand tonight. Besides, don't you think you need to keep your eyes on that wild sister of yours? God knows what shit she'll get herself into tonight."

"I already laid down the ground rules. She's playing the beautiful little hostess and keeping the fuck out of the kink tents. That's the deal." He scowled.

I chuckled. "Good luck with that shit."

"I got it covered." Twitch puffed out his chest. "She respects my big-brother swagger."

"Uh-huh." I lifted a brow.

"You're just grouchy because Hope hasn't shown up yet."

"Fuck you, Twitch," I hissed before storming away. I was even more pissed when I heard Twitch's mirth.

I stuck to the edges of the main room but still commanded the attention of every male and female while discreetly scanning the crowd.

Dammit! No sign of Hope.

I tried not to snarl while slicing through the crowd, ignoring the blatant hopeful stares women gave me. There was no shortage of women during my lifetime, but I was picky about who I took to my bed. I had a distinct taste in the bedroom, and there weren't a lot of women who could satisfy me or understand vanilla sex wasn't my cup of tea.

And I was willing to play with one woman tonight . . . and for the rest of my life.

Hope was that woman.

My tiger roared inside my head with his approval.

Yep, Hope was the only woman who could make my pulse race and, at the same time, annoy the shit out of me.

Then, just like that, she strolled into the space. Her body moved like a panther—sexy, determined, and confident. No other woman could compare to her beauty tonight.

Damn. I love her.

From the moment I'd met her, when her alluring scent had wafted into my nostrils, I'd known she was the woman who could tame the beast within me. But it was frustrating as hell that our flirting over the year hadn't amounted to anything.

Only luscious Hope could tempt me to settle down into a committed relationship. If she only understood I was willing to lay down my life to make her happy . . .

Hope stopped in her tracks, peering around like a deer in headlights. She tried to act tough, but every so often, I'd catch a glimpse of her vulnerability. She wore her hair pulled back into a tight ponytail, emphasizing her high cheekbones, bow-shaped full lips, and tip-tilted nose. Yep, this woman definitely turned heads. But it was her eyes—her strange blue eyes that contrasted against her glowing rich ebony skin—that drew me in.

There were times when, I swore, she gave off Others vibes, but nothing about her specifically smelled shifter- or vampire-like. But I knew there was no way she was human.

But what exactly was she?

Frankly, it wasn't important. The only thing I cared about was making her mine by getting her naked and well fucked in my bed—a vision I was determined to make a reality tonight. It was an image I'd replayed over and over since the first day I'd met her a year ago. At first, she'd been skittish around me. Then, as the months had progressed, we'd moved to a little bit of inno-cent flirting, but she avoided spending too much time alone with me. Even after a year, I still didn't know her any better. In fact, she did everything in her power to hide anything about herself from me.

But, tonight, Hope was an enigma I was determined to solve.

❧ 8 ❧

HOPE

Harper swayed toward me and was as gorgeous as ever in a totally sheer cutout jumpsuit that accentuated her sensuous body. How she'd gotten that thing on, I'd never know, but she looked incredible.

Harper kissed my cheek. "Thank goodness you're here."

I kissed her back. "Traffic was crazy," I replied casually, snagging a canapé from a passing waiter. "I'm okay. Stop worrying." I ate the hors d'oeuvre in one bite. "I don't want anything dampening your fun tonight."

Underneath her happy-go-lucky demeanor, Harper was fiercely protective of those she loved. I didn't want her night marred with thoughts of Carter or Others.

I looped my arm through hers, pulling her through the crowd. "So tell me about this night of pure carnal lust you've planned."

She pointed to several double doors peppered around the room. "I decided to do something different for tonight's event—you know, little rooms of pleasure to give the guests options of what they'd liked to enjoy in the name of"—she did air quotes—"'charity.'"

We stopped at a door manned by two well-dressed burly men. They pushed open the door, giving us entry.

"Here's where the dance-off will be held." She strolled with me in tow toward the three mini stages dotting the center of the large room. Three carved mahogany King Lion gothic throne chairs surrounded each stage.

"Okay, so how does this strip-a-thon work?" I inquired.

"There's no stripping involved. It's really a bump-and-grind show that's more burlesque in nature, with each dancer commanding her subjects—the men who will be sitting around each stage." Harper winked at me. "I'm calling this event The Alpha Takeover."

"Uh-huh," I replied, giving her a side eye glare that said, *I'm not buying what you're selling.*

"Most of the men here tonight are leaders. Let's call them alphas. And, in my world, alphas have all the power."

"Did you just say 'in your world'? Exactly, how much have you had to drink tonight?"

Harper jabbed me in the side. "Are you going to let me finish?"

I gestured grandly with my hand. "Go on, Queen of the Cray-Cray."

"Each dancer taking the stage will literally have these alphas at her feet to command as she sees fit. It's a play on the fact that women really have the control over men and can command them if she wields her power well." She pointed to the widescreen discreetly anchored near the ceiling. "When an alpha likes what he sees, he'll press a button to bid on the woman. Each woman will dance for thirty minutes, and the starting bid is fifty thousand dollars. Once the music stops, whoever is the highest bidder at that time wins and gets to have drinks with the dancer after the show."

I scowled at her. "Drinks only, right?" It seemed way too clean cut for the amount of money these men would have to bid to win.

Harper rolled her eyes. "I'm not a babysitter. Whatever happens between two consenting adults is none of my damn business."

"Harper"—a man frantically waved his arm from the back of the room—"we need to get started."

Damn. It's time for the extravaganza to begin.

I DIDN'T EVEN RECOGNIZE MYSELF IN THE HUGE FLOOR MIRROR tucked into the corner. For my performance, I wanted to go for a clean, fresh face with a bit of attitude and pizazz. When I danced, I would try to portray a lot through facial expressions, so I refreshed my cat eyes and red lips.

A knock on the door sounded loudly, and Harper peeped in. Her eyes widened. "Damn, those boots are made for strutting."

I'd decided to pair my racy stage ensemble with red PVC thigh-high boots. "Don't start. I'm freaking out here. I haven't done a solo onstage in years. But here I am, about to shake my moneymaker"—I did air quotes—"'for the alphas.'"

Harper smiled, dramatically blinking her eyelashes. "But it's for the children. Just think of all the families you'll provide with affordable homes by shaking that ass. Besides, it will be an enriching experience . . . for all involved."

My fingers clenched. "Then why the hell don't you do it?" I mumbled under my breath.

"Because someone has to be the ringmaster of this circus, and that's me," she responded flatly.

Harper eyed my black bodysuit that bared it all. I was showing off tons of cleavage in the skintight leotard, but the front seemed modest in comparison to my naked bum, covered only by nude fishnet tights.

"Damn, that's hot. When you take the stage, those alphas are not going to know what hit them."

I ignored her while stretching and chanting to myself, "Remember, it's for the children."

Harper chuckled.

I gave her the evil eye. "Harper, this isn't funny. I'm going to make an ass of myself. It's been years since I've really *danced* just for the fun of it. I don't even have a routine planned." That was scary and exciting. "And what song am I going to dance to?" My mind was racing.

Now I was really annoyed at myself for freaking out. I wasn't even a panic kind of girl.

"Don't worry about it. I got your song picked out, and it's a banger." She suggestively danced around me. "By the way, the alphas caught one glimpse of you downstairs, and they have been drooling . . . especially Elijah." She bopped her head around, her blond hair wildly flying through the air. "Maybe tonight, he'll finally get lucky and have the privilege of tapping that ass." She swatted my butt.

Smiling sweetly, I stepped forward and proceeded to wrap my hands around her neck in a playful choke, and she lightheartedly gagged.

"Will you stop fucking around? I'm really stressed here," I groaned.

Totally ignoring me, she eyed the clock. "We've got to go. It's almost time for me to MC this motherfucker."

I barely had a chance to snatch my black knee-length trench coat before she hustled me out of the room and down the stairs. We entered some backstage area with two scantily dressed stick-thin women with obviously fake breasts—one redhead, the other brunette—as sensuous music whirled around me, like a prelude to the main event.

Harper clapped her hands to get our attention. "Okay, ladies, here's how it's going to work. Each act will dance to the same song for thirty minutes. I'll call you out, one by one, and you grab whatever stage you deem fit. There are only three chairs per stage, and the alphas will bid on the dancer they're interested in. That's all."

The redhead examined me with her lips curled into a sneer. "I guess chubby is the new thing this year."

The other woman snickered. "Poor thing won't get a bid. Don't waste your time, sweetie."

Harper moved toward them with clenched fists "Why, you little . . ."

I snatched Harper back. "Nope, don't do it." I shot them a disdainful glare. "All the fighting will be handled out there, onstage, where it matters." And I was planning on handing out two resounding dance slaps, Brooklyn-style, to each of them.

The music lowered.

"Showtime!" Harper exclaimed, clipping on her microphone. Pushing aside the heavy silk curtains, she sauntered across the floor.

I counted at least thirty men of every ethnic background and age standing around, not one of them sitting in the chairs.

"Good evening, alphas!" Harper shouted. "Who's ready to have some fun tonight?" she purred.

Some of the men whistled and clapped.

"Well, all right. Tonight, we have three beautiful women, handpicked personally by me, to rock your world." She strolled up to where the DJ was situated and smiled prettily. "Let's just have fun and put aside the animosity between us for one night. As you know, Ryker couldn't be here tonight, but he's here in spirit. He created this tradition of gathering together as a way for us to unite without the petty bickering over supremacy."

Harper continued. "The rules tonight are really simple. You've already paid for access to this throne room." She gestured dramatically with a wave of her hand. "But if you want to take the throne"—she pointed to the three chairs surrounding each stage—"you bid on the dancer you're interested in. When the music stops, the highest bidder wins."

She pointed to the DJ. "Let's get this party started."

The sensuous heavy beat of the music thumped and echoed throughout the room.

"Alphas, I'm pleased to introduce the lovely fox, Layla; the tantalizing cheetah, Sofia; and the simply scrumptious, Queen Hope."

Layla and Sofia swayed out with their heads held high. I froze, letting the familiar performance jitters course through my body, before the adrenaline took over.

I watched Layla, the gorgeous brunette, flouncing across the stage with a feather fan twirling around her body. Three men instantly took the chairs surrounding her stage. Sofia took her stage with a confidence I couldn't help but admire. Her movements were sensual and evocative as she twisted her body. Frankly, I'd never seen anything so seductive.

"Come on out, Queen Hope," Harper called out. "Show these alphas how you do it."

Turning up the collar of my trench coat, I slipped into my stage persona, giving myself the courage to be free and sexy while performing. I strutted toward the third stage with a deliberate sway to my hips. My gaze swept to every man as a hush filled the room. Unleashed dominance pulsed around me. Seductively licking my lips, I coyly gazed at them from under my eyelashes. Releasing all the tension, my body relaxed, fully taking in the magnitude of the utter power and hotness of my captive audience.

A man with black hair winked at me. "Simply gorgeous," he praised with a drawl.

Yep, I could do this, judging from the lustful, hooded stares of the men who were now observing me with the utmost attention.

Placing one foot directly in front of the other, I strutted over, skirting to a stop when two men got up from the chairs surrounding Layla's stage and decidedly sat in the chairs surrounding mine. I continued my swagger.

The music and atmosphere were liberating. I was the queen,

and these men were my subjects, where I could control them in any way I wanted. But none of them was the man I wanted to command. I glanced at the widescreen. The bid was at $100,000 for me, and I hadn't even taken the stage yet.

Elijah smoothly stepped out of the shadows and took the third chair at my stage. Lifting his glass to his lips, he pensively regarded me.

Now the real show can begin.

Instead of taking the stairs to the stage, I approached his chair. Lifting his chin with a finger, I leaned in with my lips close, as if I were going to kiss him, and then I stopped. "You're late," I purred. I lightly pushed his head back, shooting him a seductive smile.

His eyes narrowed with desire. "I'm right on time, it seems," he muttered, "to claim what's mine. Now show me exactly what I'm getting for my money."

My heart raced from the challenge.

"Alpha, this is my show, and I'm in complete control. Now sit there and behave."

When I extended my hand to him, he wrapped his arms around me, effortlessly lifting me onto the stage with a hard tap on the ass in parting.

I had a good view of Layla's and Sofia's stages, and there were no men sitting in the chairs. The two women became livid, storming off the stages and out of the room. Now all the men were standing around my stage, as if willing the three men who occupied the chairs to get up and allow them to sit.

"All right, Queen Hope is commanding the alphas. Let's go, men. Who wants her bad enough to take the highest bid?" Harper demanded.

With my back facing Elijah, I unbuttoned my coat, beginning at the top. I glanced over at one of the men occupying a seat at the stage and continued unbuttoning.

Harper announced, "Victor has the high bid at one hundred thirty thousand."

I slightly raised my shoulder so the jacket slid down a little bit, exposing my skin. Extracting both arms from the sleeves, I gradually let the jacket drop, tossing it off the stage.

"It's getting hot in here. Damien's bid one hundred sixty thousand," Harper crowed. "Victor's bid one hundred ninety thousand."

I poised dramatically before twirling around in a quarter circle, and then I added a booty shake. I made sure to stay nice and low when I bounced again, accentuating an ass only covered by nude fishnet tights.

Knowing no man could resist my secret weapon—the booty roll—I slid onto all fours with my knees apart and circled my butt around in a figure-eight shape. I sat back on my feet with my knees together and then stood, one leg at a time, before shaking my hips. I snapped off the band holding my hair into a ponytail and swung my head around, unleashing a cloud of hair. Strutting across the stage, abruptly I stopped at the sight of the men blatantly giving Elijah challenging glares.

"Fuck off, she's mine," Elijah gritted out. "Two hundred twenty thousand dollars," he shouted right before the music stopped.

I blinked when I swore his eyes became more feline as his hand clenched his glass.

"Winning bid is two hundred twenty thousand. Elijah is the winning bid," Harper announced.

The men surrounding my stage drifted away, including the two men sitting in the chairs.

The DJ started playing a slow song. Extending my hand to Elijah, I demanded, "Take my hand, alpha."

He grasped my hand, and using his hard thigh as a step stool, I advanced down onto the floor. Snaking myself around his body before standing between his wide-open legs, I dipped forward, brushing my breasts against his chest.

His face was like granite. No emotions showed as his hands clenched and unclenched, like he was fighting the need to touch me. I twirled around, giving him my back, and I started a slow sway of my hips from side to side. Upping the ante, my butt moved in circles as it hovered over his crotch.

I caressed his hot, hard length before whispering, "Someone's enjoying the show."

I lowered myself onto his lap, grinding against his body and looking back at him over my shoulder. "And there it begins—the gnashing of teeth. Someone is a little too tense. Let me help you relax." I bounced my ass onto his cock and then held it over, not touching him.

His fingers trailed along my arm, sending chills up and down my spine.

"Now, it's not nice to tease an alpha on the edge of making you get on your knees in public." He nipped my ear, hard.

My hot sheath clenched with desire at the thought of me on my knees and at his mercy. "That sounds . . . promising."

"Then I look forward to showing you exactly what I have in store for you." His tongue flicked my neck.

Pulling away from him, I strolled up the stairs with a booty shake on each stair. I spun around to study him one more time before the music ended.

MY HAIR FLOWED around my shoulders, and the gown swayed against my ankles. I was giddy, strolling into the room with a fully intoxicated Harper talking excitedly about my performance. With her arm looped through mine, she was practically skipping like a schoolgirl.

"That was the most fun I've had in a while, and it's the highest amount raised for this party," Harper boasted.

As I grabbed a glass of champagne from a passing waiter, my mouth twisted sardonically. "Well, that's what happens when you underestimate the power of a curvy, sexy ass," I responded.

The strobe lights flickered against the skin of the barely dressed women and men gyrating along the stage as if their lives depended on it. Partiers were too busy grinding against each other on the dance floor as the beat of the music thrummed seductively. The room was so dark all I could see were bits and pieces of body parts doing obscene things that were better left in the bedroom.

I had to admit it. "This party is fucking amazing," I whispered under my breath.

Glancing around, I pretended not to be searching for Elijah. My body pulsed with arousal when I found him making his way through the crowd. Biting my bottom lip, I gave him a slow once-over.

"Damn, he sure knows how to make cunts wet without even trying," I blurted.

As if he felt me eye-fucking him, he pivoted and stared at me, his eyes smoldering with intensity. Shamelessly, I drank in the magnificence of Elijah like a thirsty woman in a desert. While he observed me, my heart was beating like I'd just run fifty miles in thirty seconds.

I want to lick every inch of him.

Three words described Elijah—hot, sexy, and panty-dropping.

As I looked from his tailored black slacks that molded against his sculptured thighs to the crisp black shirt that fit across his magnificent broad chest, my panties were soaked and my nipples were as hard as rocks. With deliberate effort, I broke eye contact with him.

Harper stared at me. "Jesus, why don't you two just get a tent?"

I eyed her right back. "I owe him a drink only." My mouth grew dry.

"There's no shame in admitting you want him. He's hot but a little rough around the edges." Her full lips pursed. "So are you finally going to do it?" she asked, peering at me from the side of her eye with a smirk.

I lifted the champagne glass to my lips, continuing to stare at my sinful fixation. "Do what?"

"Oh, for fuck's sake!" Harper jabbed me in the side. "You're licking the rim of your glass while undressing him with your eyes."

Shit!

My tongue stopped mid twirl. I hadn't even realized I'd been doing it.

Dammit!

I needed to get this obsession under control. Just the sight of him made me do the most out-of-character things.

I scowled at her before draining my glass and placing it on the tray of the passing damn near nude waiter before snatching another glass.

"Jesus, what the hell am I doing here?" I mumbled under my breath.

Harper hip-checked me while wiggling her body to the thumping beat of the music. "You're breaking out of vanilla hell and walking onto the wild side of play. Welcome to my world." She winked.

As usual, Harper's bubbly personality was infectious.

"Got it." I smirked before hip-checking her back.

She smacked a kiss on my cheek.

"So, in essence, this party is your personal freaky play-ground." Grabbing her hips, I swayed to the music.

The partiers curiously considered us. I didn't blame them. Harper and I were just so similar. She was tall, curvy, and blond. I was statuesque with a tight, shapely body that had more ass and breasts than should be allowed, with exotic dark features and long, jet-black hair. She was perky and optimistic, and I was streetwise pessimistic. But Harper was the one person, my partner in crime, to whom I couldn't say no. She was my only best friend, and when she needed me, I would be there, just like she was there for me. It had been that way from the first day we'd met, and it would always be that way.

She pouted prettily. "Yes, it's my pleasure house, which I can't fully enjoy, not with Twitch watching me like some damn prison guard."

"Uh, what did you expect? He's doing security for his baby sister's kinky party. It's awkward all around."

Harper scowled. "I had no choice. None of the guests would RSVP until I guaranteed tight security. They were bitching about ensuring their safety. Blah, blah, blah." She dramatically waved her hand as she smiled at a pretty woman on the dance floor. "To make matters worse, now Twitch and Elijah are all uptight about your incident."

My back stiffened, and my eyes narrowed. "Oh, hell no! You told them my damn business?"

Harper's eyes snapped back to me with a wild, panicked stare. "I had to. They were with me when you called. You were hysterical, which is very unusual for you, and it only made me hysterical. So when Elijah asked what was going on . . ." She shrugged. "He's ex-military. Years in special operations have honed his interrogation skills. Sorry, I folded like a deck of cards." She shot him a dirty look. "Damn bastard."

I gritted my teeth. That was why I'd hesitated in calling her, but I had been so freaked out that all common sense went flying out the window. "That's no excuse, Harper."

She knew how private I was, and I damn sure didn't need super-macho Elijah hovering around me like some protective warrior. Absently, I rubbed the scar between my breasts, fighting the urge to run out of the party and back to the safety of my townhouse. But I refused to let Carter win . . . again. I could protect myself.

Harper grabbed my arm. "Don't get all huffy. I was worried."

"What else did you tell him?" I demanded.

"What?" Her eyes widened. "I wouldn't tell him that. I would go to my grave with what you confided in me."

I breathed out, allowing my body to relax. *What was wrong with me?* I knew she wouldn't divulge the deep, dark secret about what Carter had tried to do to me.

"I know you wouldn't."

I watched as a famous actress led three guys into the tent reserved for those who wanted to get their freak on in private.

"You know me. I'm far from a prude, and I'm damn sure all for getting your kink on . . . but this is an all-out celebrity orgy."

"It's not an orgy. If you want to play, that's all good, but it's optional," Harper said.

"These are not my type of people."

"This is the hall of fame of fantasies," Harper retorted. "Live a little. Say yes to Elijah."

"Absolutely not. Just one drink because that's what he paid for, but that's it," I returned flatly.

"Uh-huh," Harper uttered.

I exhaled heavily, eyeballing him from across the room.

Elijah was magnificent.

His searing amber eyes made me seriously horny. His body was pure rippling muscle, and he had to be at least six three. And his gravelly low voice . . . well, I couldn't count on both hands the hot, wet dreams I'd had with that voice whispering freaky shit as he made love to me.

Elijah stopped to talk to Twitch, and as if he could sense my heated stare, he arched a brow at me. There was no smile. He crossed his muscular arms as my gaze traveled up his tall body, stopping at his piercing eyes.

God. He's ice-cream-cone lickable.

I clenched my fingers, wanting so badly to run them through his hair.

Shit. Shit. Shit.

It was going to be another long night of pushing my vibrator to the breaking point.

Harper shook her head. "You two have been circling each other like sharks for a year. Will one of you just submit so you can fuck this thing out? I'm exhausted of the tension around you two."

I tiredly ran my hands through my hair, trying not to show my anxiousness. "If only I could," I mumbled under my breath.

"Hope, believe me, Elijah can take on Carter any day of the week. It breaks my fucking heart that you're letting that freak Carter rob you of a relationship with Elijah. Just open up to him and come clean."

Twitch smirked while saying something to Elijah. He shrugged his wide shoulders before Twitch walked away.

I did agree with Harper about the tension. For some reason,

it was getting worse, like a rubber band about to snap. But I guessed that was what you got when two dominant personalities collided—total anarchy.

Elijah was watching me with hooded eyes.

I swallowed hard, trying not to squirm under his sensuous stare.

I nudged Harper with my elbow. "What's up with him tonight?" my voice croaked.

"Go find out." She shoved me forward.

I shot her an annoyed scowl before handing her my glass.

"Tell the big, bad tiger I said hi," Harper retorted before winking at me.

I strolled through the crowd, ignoring the interested stares of men. Stopping in front of Elijah, I anxiously licked my bottom lip at the strange waves of energy rolling off him.

"What do you want?" I asked.

His eyes moved from my face to my body and then back again. "The question is, do you know what you want?" His eyes flickered from the party's light. "Because I do."

I had to cross my legs as my sex clenched with need. His nose twitched.

"And that is?" My chin lifted.

His amber eyes glinted. "To submit," he growled as his hands grabbed my waist, pulling me to his obvious arousal.

I glanced away, watching the couples sway to the rhythm of the song playing.

My gaze snapped back when Elijah leaned down and whispered in my ear, "You want to dance?"

I remained stubbornly silent.

"It's a dance, Hope. I'm not asking to fuck you . . . yet."

Elijah grabbed my hand in one motion, pulling me through the crowd. He stopped where the shadows enclosed us. The sea of grinding bodies danced all around us in various states of undress. He turned, cupping my hips with his huge palms. I tried to pull back, but he held me still, giving my hips a light squeeze.

I gasped as Elijah pulled me tightly against him.

With his lips inches from my ear, he spoke softly to me. "All I can think about right now is pulling up your dress and slipping my cock in, taking you right here."

The power of his words made my toes curl in my stilettos.

"Fuck, that's hot." The breathless response slipped out before I could stop it.

When one hand slid to my ass like it belonged there, I knew I was in big trouble. He felt way too good.

Staring, mesmerized, I watched Elijah's other hand reach out, his big fingers sliding across my cheek. His calloused thumb dragged across my bottom lip. I jerked at the contact.

"Don't move," he demanded.

His hand slid to my jaw, and his head tilted before his lips settled across my mouth. My breath caught, as I was undecided on whether to pull back or allow him to delve farther. I soon realized there was no allowing; Elijah was going to claim me. His grip on my jaw tightened. His tongue slid between my teeth. His kiss was long and slow—the stamp of his possession. No one had ever kissed me like this.

Jesus, I'm so fucked.

I moaned. The damn man tasted like a delicious combination of mint and hot chocolate.

He plunged ahead, his tongue curling around mine, demanding it to come out and play. That was when all hell broke out. Need swirled in my stomach, a desire that only Elijah could satisfy. We both groaned, and my eyes slid closed. My stomach tightened as a rush of heat flooded my entire body. My hands wrapped tightly around his lean waist. Lust coiled deep inside me.

My heart raced. Elijah felt right, like he now belonged to me. Tears swelled behind my eyelids. I was overwhelmed with emotions I'd worked so hard to bury.

He pulled his mouth away from mine but kept his hand firmly controlling my face before slowly releasing it.

He spun our bodies in a circle and stopped right in front of a tent with a couple standing inside. Their bodies were wrapped around one another. Their breathing harsh, their mouths erotically licking and sucking in the most passionate kiss I'd ever seen. Their focus was completely on each other.

My muscles locked, leaving me paralyzed. "I can't watch."

"Why? Don't you like the way his mouth is fucking hers?" He turned me around to face the couple. My back pressed against his chest.

That was the problem. I liked watching way too much. But it wasn't just the act of me watching. It was also Elijah's presence and the way his body was pressed against mine. His touch, his smell, his voice were doing things to my body, driving me toward the edge of insanity.

"Hope, touch yourself," Elijah whispered as he pressed his large palms against my breasts before falling away and settling on my hips.

I shook my head and tried to move away, but Elijah stopped me.

"No, don't." He shifted his stance, his thighs spread wide on either side of my legs. His cock nudged the small of my back. His scent of earth and sandalwood engulfed me.

A wave of arousal washed over me. "Oh God," I breathed, nearly lightheaded from pleasure.

He ran a finger down my cheek before pressing his thumb into my mouth. I ran my tongue around his thumb. He groaned with pleasure. I spun around, plunging my fingers into his hair, scraping his scalp with wild abandon.

"I want you," he murmured.

I bit back a whimper.

He traced the cleft of my ass. "I could make you come, Hope."

I peeked around to see if anyone was watching us, but it was so dark, and everyone was busy with their own scandalous escapades that they couldn't give a shit about what we were doing.

"No," I answered, even as my hips rolled, nearing orgasm.

"Ask me, Hope. Ask me to release that storm brewing between your legs." His erotic challenge licked at my clitoris, and it jerked in response.

"Elijah . . ."

"Stop fucking thinking," he growled in my ear as he burrowed his fingers into my hair and jerked hard.

My sex pulsed as his grip tightened. Longing coiled so hard my stomach clenched. He jerked my head again.

Out of nowhere, a familiar scent wafted through the air . . . Carter's sickly sweet odor. My heart raced.

Oh God, Carter is here.

The memory of the way Carter's eyes had morphed into a feral crimson red as he hacked away at Troy, like a butcher disassembling a slab of meat, rushed through my mind. My head snapped back as I tried to pull away.

Elijah's grip tightened. "Don't move, Hope."

"No," I gasped, wrenching out of his hold. I stumbled back a step, my heart thundering in my chest.

Carter was here, and he was going to kill Elijah.

"Elijah, I've got to go." My sacrifice was my happiness. I loved Elijah too much to let him get killed.

"Hope!" he shouted.

It filled me with dread that he was fighting so hard for me and for us. But it was selfish of me to want him.

I dodged his attempt to stop me, skirting away and weaving through the gyrating crowd, heading for the entrance. I almost made it to the door when I felt his muscular arms wrap around me. Involuntarily, I sank into his body.

"Don't ever run away from me, Hope," Elijah's dark voice whispered in my ear.

The muscles in my body went still, rebelling at his dominant tone and grip. When a flashback of the night Carter had grabbed and shoved me entered my mind, I panicked and stiffened like a statue.

Elijah spun me around and silently stared at me. "I'm not him, Hope."

My eyes lowered briefly before locking onto him. "I don't know what you're talking about."

"Don't ever fucking lie to me. If you're not ready to talk about it, I'll let it go . . . for now. But I won't allow you to taint the trust I'm trying to build."

My body tensed. "Trust? Let's get something straight, Elijah. I will not deny I want you," I admitted with more steel in my voice than I actually felt. "But we are not building anything. Got me?"

He leaned closer, whispering, "Oh, I get it. I get I scare the shit out of you. But understand this. I'm not going anywhere. I'm tired of waiting for you to open your eyes and see the man who's willing to give you everything you need. This man." He pointed at himself.

His words thrummed through my body. My traitorous flesh was under his control.

"That's not going to happen."

"Believe me, Hope. It will. You will be mine—mind, body, and soul—and that is a fucking fact," he replied. "And to prove I know you so well, I'll tell you exactly how this night is going to play out. I will make you come, hard, and you will push me away and run away with your tail between your legs. I will allow you to run, and I won't chase you. And do you know why?" He cocked his head, desire flaring in his eyes.

My nails dug into his forearms. "Why?" I whispered.

"Because you will come back to me of your own free will. In your heart, you know you belong to me and I to you." His voice lowered.

My arousal beat at me hard. The truth of his words hit home.

"Dammit. You're not making this easy, Elijah."

He cupped my face, cradling my jaw with one hand while the

other grabbed the back of my neck. "Love is not easy," his sexy low voice whispered over my skin.

I shivered.

"Love is pure, dirty, and raw. Give me one night, Hope. No inhibitions. No fears. Just you and me, right here, right now." He leaned in with his lips brushing my ear.

My body trembled deliciously with passion swirling in my moist needy place. *Just to have him for one night . . .*

My fingers wrapped around his bicep. I nodded, allowing him to back me up into an empty tent behind us. He closed the curtains.

I shut my eyes, sinking into the couch.

"Open your eyes." His rough growl stroked my skin.

I groaned, hesitating.

"Now, Hope." His voice hardened.

Trembling, I opened my eyes.

His eyes were like dark amber. "Stand up and take off your dress." His legs widened as he rolled up the sleeves of his crisp black shirt, displaying the tattoos covering his forearms.

On shaky legs, I stood up, reached over to my side, and unzipped the dress. I tugged the dress down and stood before him wearing nothing but my stilettos and black lace bra and panties.

Oh God, Hope, what are you doing?

This was so out of the norm for me, but here I was, standing before Elijah, my body exposed to the cold air.

"Damn, you're so sexy," he praised.

His words unleashed the dam of emotions. This was Elijah—a man I'd known for a year and secretly lusted after from the first moment I had seen him.

Slowly, I took off my lingerie and then raised one leg onto the couch, giving him the full view of my ass. I bent to take off my shoes.

"No. Leave them on," he barked.

I placed my foot back onto the floor. Right now, all that

mattered was finally having Elijah. I reached up and cupped my breasts, squeezing my hardened nipples between my fingers.

His eyes dilated as he stepped forward, pulling me to him. "Is that what you want, Hope? Pain?"

I bit my full bottom lip, groaning at the sweet lust whipping through my dripping sex. In a flash, I found myself pressed face-down onto the couch with him wedged against my back. His cock still covered by his pants rested on my ass. My palms slapped against the couch as I pushed back onto his erection, grinding against it.

The music reverberated against the booth. Inhibitions flew out the door.

Elijah pulled away, and the cool air kissed the backs of my thighs, the globes of my ass, and the wetness of my sex.

He ran a hand across the curve of my ass before parting it. A shiver ran down my spine. This should have made me squirm from embarrassment. I was lying there, butt naked and vulnerable to Elijah's eyes and touch, and I absolutely loved it.

I'd only had one lover after Carter, and that experience was a disaster because I'd had a panic attack right in the middle of sex. After that, I'd resigned myself to a life of sex toys to satisfy my urges.

Yet here I was, allowing Elijah to take me and see me in ways no other man had. My eyes closed at the revelation.

✳ 10 ✳

ELIJAH

MY TIGER WAS CLAWING FURIOUSLY to get out.

Hope belonged to me.

The gauntlet had been thrown. I would do everything in my power to keep her by my side forever.

Damn, I'm never letting her go.

She was everything I wanted and more. Her beautiful ebony skin glowed. She was mine for the taking, but I had no intention of having our first time be here. No, it would be at my penthouse, secluded, where I would fuck her for days with no interruption, and then I'd claim her.

Tonight was just a teaser of things to come.

My hands skimmed over her thighs. My cock surged, pressing against the zipper of my pants. She gasped. The muscles in her ass flexed and relaxed under my caress.

"Elijah," she whispered. Her voice was uncertain. "I . . ."

"Relax," I soothed, pressing a lingering kiss to the back of her neck. "I'll always take care of you, Hope. Just let go of your fears."

I flipped her over and gripped her hips. Moving one hand over her stomach, I slid it down slightly. Hope's breath caught. I paused. I wanted this moment to last forever, but I needed to press her further.

My fingers trailed down and burrowed between her thighs. A cry escaped from her luscious lips, and her husky groan pierced the air. I pressed my fingers into her wet slit. Her soft flesh enveloped me as I gently moved back and forth into her sex.

"You're soaking wet with need." I circled her clit.

"Wait." She panted. "Don't." Her hand grabbed my wrist.

With a controlled motion, I flicked her sex, hard. Hope's eyes rolled back as she let out a loud moan. My cock throbbed.

"You want me to stop?" I didn't stop, sliding my fingers inside her folds, slowly going in and out.

Her hips followed my movements in a sensual rhythm that drove me insane.

"Hope?" I parted her folds, rubbing her sensitive channel. "Answer me." My voice hardened, and my movements stilled.

She pressed up, trying to make my fingers resume. I refused to give in. I wanted her reply—now.

"You'd better answer, Hope," I commanded.

"Don't you dare stop, Elijah," she snarled. She pressed my fingers to her junction and gyrated against it.

This was going further than I'd anticipated, but I couldn't stop. I plunged my fingers into her core and pumped hard and fast.

"Oh . . . shit . . ." she cried out with her body arched.

She purred like a sexy kitten. The sound strummed against my balls.

"Fuck," I growled. "Hope, you are so fucking sexy."

Her glistening moist folds trembled around my fingers. Her hips bucked under my touch. She was close to release, so I pushed her closer to the edge by sliding and pinching her nub.

"Wait." Hope stiffened. "Don't stop." Her neck arched. "Go, dammit!" A scream of ecstasy escaped. She convulsed, and her sex pulsed under my touch.

I continued to fuck her, riding her through the orgasm,

giving her all she craved. Her flesh contracted as I withdrew my fingers.

I'd never wanted a woman like I desired Hope. It was foreign and new. But I wasn't afraid to surrender to it.

Her head sagged to the side in exhaustion, baring her neck and the juncture where I would someday mark her as mine. I leaned forward, raining kisses on her neck and shoulders. Her body was still shuddering from the orgasm. Her face glowed with satisfaction. She looked so innocent, vulnerable, with all her normal guards down.

This was the woman I wanted—the woman who wasn't afraid to let me in.

I stared down at her ample cleavage and then arched down, kissing the scar between it. I was determined to heal this woman, erasing the emotional wounds that fucker had left.

I knew getting Hope's ultimate surrender was going to be rough, but I was in it for the long haul.

She was mine—whether she knew it or not.

❧ II ❧

HOPE

"HOW DID YOU GET THIS SCAR?" Elijah boomed.

My eyes snapped open and my breath caught. "I don't want to talk about it."

I shoved him. He stiffened before rolling away and standing up.

I jumped to my feet, and with jerky movements, I tugged on my lingerie and dress, avoiding eye contact.

The beat of the music was loud, reminding me of the crowd partying outside. I felt his body pressed against my back when I was fully dressed.

"Why?" Elijah asked from behind.

"I've got to go," I snapped, heading toward the exit.

"This is bullshit." He reached out, cuffing my upper arm, halting my dash out of the tent.

I snatched my arm free. Gently gripping my other arm, he spun me around. I swallowed hard, trying not to panic while fighting the all-familiar dread that seeped into my bones. Logically, I knew he was nothing like Carter, but something in me broke.

The memories lingered. The fear remained.

And nothing could erase the psychological stains, remnants

of Carter's multiple attacks on me—not thousands of dollars spent while baring my soul on my therapist's sofa, not hundreds of sweaty hours of self-defense classes, and not even my love for Elijah.

I was an emotionally broken woman.

"Let me go, Elijah," I stammered.

He cupped my jaw. His calloused palm pressed against my skin. I struggled not to cave to his erotic caress that sent jolts down to my clit. His thumb slowly swept across my full bottom lip.

"Tell me what happened."

"It's none of your damn business," I stated, cringing at my hoarse tone.

"You are my damn business," he seethed as his hand tightened on my jaw. "Someone tried to kill you, and I want to know who and why."

I felt the tears threatening to fall. *Show no weakness, Hope.*

Elijah leaned forward until our foreheads met. His moist breath brushed across my lips.

"Tell me why you won't open up to me, Hope. That scar is the past. I am the future. Let it go."

My heart raced with fear. "That's the whole point. The past isn't the past, not with a man I dated briefly, Carter, out of the mental hospital and stalking me." My body shivered with disgust as I remembered how the utter madness had spiraled out of control after I'd broken up with Carter. "He will never leave me alone. He's proven that many times over."

Elijah was no stranger. He deserved to know the truth and what he would be dealing with if he wanted to be with me.

"Carter tried to kill me. I was naive and flattered that a man like him—handsome, rich, intelligent—was so attracted to me."

"Any man should be grateful to have you in his life, Hope."

"I know that now, but back then, I was really young and searching for self-validation in all the wrong men." I scoffed.

"And what had started out as a dream relationship ended as a horror movie."

Elijah's eyes clouded with sympathy.

I pushed on. "After I broke up with him, the craziness started. He bombarded me with hundreds of texts and emails. He relentlessly followed me while I was on a world tour with a client. He stalked me, stalked my friends. His parents turned it all around and accused me of ruining their son." I swallowed hard. "I reported him to the police. He pleaded guilty to harassment, and I thought his reign of terror was over."

Elijah's fists tightened at his sides. "That fucker," he snarled.

I touched his arm. "Let me finish, because if I don't get this all out now, I never will." I took a deep breath. "Carter attacked me twice. The first time was when I decided to attend a friend's birthday party at a club. I went to the restroom, and when I came out of the stall, Carter was standing there, blocking the exit. Before I could escape, he grabbed me, pulling me into a restroom stall with a knife pressed against my throat. He babbled words of love over and over as he brutally ripped off my clothes with sick lust in his eyes."

Elijah pulled me into his chest, wrapping his beefy arms around me.

I recalled the feeling of total hopelessness that I'd felt that night when seeing Carter's crazed stare. Bitterness had coated my tongue when I realized I was nothing but a piece of property to him. He viewed me as his possession that he had every intention of claiming over and over again until I broke.

Tears streamed down my face as I braced for Carter's impending savage violation. Shivering, I turned my head away, letting my mind go blank. I knew I would never be the same after he was done. But when the door slammed open and I heard excited voices of women talking, I was thrown a lifeline. I screamed at the top of my lungs, and Carter released me with utter rage clouding his eyes before his gaze went flat and hard.

"You'll always belong to me, Hope," he hissed before coolly walking away.

My thoughts snapped back to the present when I heard Elijah's voice saying, "It will be all right now, Hope. He'll never touch you again."

"I'm not so sure, Elijah. Carter's second attack was fatal. I vividly remember that day. I had an extra pep in my step as I walked to meet my date, Troy, after finally getting an order of protection against Carter. The past was behind me, and I remained strong and steadfast, even while refusing to be pressured by his parents, who had complained I was treating their son like a criminal and he had no intention of harming me. But I knew better. Carter was unstable and refused to accept the fact that I wasn't interested in him."

There was a thickness in my throat when I continued. "Just hours after he was served with the restraining order, he casually walked into the coffee shop where I was having coffee with Troy, and he stabbed both of us. He narrowly missed my heart. Troy wasn't as lucky. He died from multiple stab wounds. So you see, Troy got killed because of me, and I refuse to have another man's blood on my conscience."

My legs trembled as I tilted my head back, needing to place some distance—emotional and physical—between us.

"He's crazy, and he should be in jail," Elijah snapped.

"Well, he's not." I shook my head. "His parents manipulated the system and got him admitted into a mental institution, claiming insanity."

His face tightened. "You don't ever have to be afraid, Hope. I can protect you."

I let out a sharp bark of laughter. "You can't protect me. No one can."

He released his hold on me and stepped back. "I know what you're doing. You're trying to push me away. You're scared."

My mouth tightened. "I'm not scared. I'm practical. And just because I allowed you to stick your fingers in my pussy doesn't make you an authority on all things Hope."

"I know you more than you care to admit. You had an abusive boyfriend who tried to kill you. I get your fear, but you can't live your life terrified. You're allowing him to win, to control your happiness and life. It's time to move on, but instead, you're punishing yourself for that asshole's actions."

His words struck a chord in my heart. I wanted to deny what he said, but I knew it was true. I was paralyzed as he stepped closer. He wrapped his arms around my body.

"Hope . . ." He tenderly grazed his lips over my temple. His gesture stirred emotions I didn't care to evaluate. "Let me in."

"I've got to go," I squeaked.

His eyes narrowed. "If that's what you want, but let's get one thing clear," he murmured. "Not all men are monsters." His tongue flicked my earlobe. "It's not about control; it's about trust—you trusting me to give you what you need," his sexy low voice whispered over my skin, causing me to shiver. "Like your need to have me licking your slick folds while you lie open, spread eagle."

Oh shit.

"How about having me balls-deep buried in your pussy?" he whispered. He pulled my hips against his rigid erection. "You need me buried so deep inside your throbbing sex that you won't know where I end and you begin."

My eyes squeezed closed as my chest heaved while I envisioned every word he'd described.

"Hope?"

My eyes snapped open to find him intensely staring at me.

Elijah knew. He saw past the walls I had painfully erected, and he was determined to tear them down, brick by brick.

"Are you afraid your ex-boyfriend will hurt me?" he asked pointedly.

"No." My shoulders stiffened. I sucked in a deep breath. "He'll kill you, and I won't survive it if he does."

"There's so much you don't know about me. I'm the most dangerous motherfucker around."

"Don't play protector. I can handle this on my own."

He roared, and it almost sounded animal-like. In a flash, my hand was enfolded in his larger one and pulled around his neck. "Everyone needs a little help." He released my hand and smoothed the pad of his thumb over my jawline. "We belong together. You know this. Let me protect you."

I yearned to take what he was offering with both hands, but desire warred with logic. Carter was out and watching, and I knew exactly what he was capable of.

Inhaling deeply, I took a step back, and Elijah's hands fell to his sides.

"Hope . . ."

"It will never work. I can't give you what you want, Elijah." My heart raced. "I'm broken, scarred, and fucking defeated. I'm not ready for a relationship."

I bit back the bitter regret. I wanted him so badly, but I had too many skeletons in my closet to try to make it work.

Elijah grabbed my wrist, roughly dragging me against him. He kissed me so tenderly but dominated me at the same time. I pulled out of his grip, frightened to fucking death.

Pivoting on my heel, I opened the curtain with emotions of sorrow and loneliness churning inside my stomach. I walked out of the tent, fighting not to glance back at him.

Stopping a waiter, I asked, "Where's the closest exit?"

He pointed. Walking through the house, I wrapped my arms around myself, and for the first time in my life, I let the salty tears of regret flow down my cheeks, unchecked.

"Dammit!" I dashed them away as I stepped into the darkened lobby.

The further I walked, the more the lighting changed, growing ominous. At the end of the passageway was an exit.

My cell rang, and I answered the call.

"Cassidy?" I frowned. It was really late for him to be calling.

"I don't know how to tell you this. Frank was killed in a drive-by shooting."

I bit my bottom lip. Tears trickled down my cheeks, and I dashed them away.

"Thank you for calling, Cassidy. Do you know who killed him?" I wanted to know if it was the demon or Carter.

"I don't know, but I'll find out, one way or another." He paused. "Carter was out the same time your uncle was killed. I don't believe in coincidences. Watch your back, Hope."

Shit. I'd left my gun at home. "I will," I replied.

Our call ended.

My heels clicked against the floor as I headed toward the exit. Pulling the door open, I stepped outside into an unlit area beside the mansion.

My cell buzzed with a text. Tapping to open it, only two words appeared—*You're next*—with a photo attached of me looking down at my cell attached. My head snapped up when I heard the idling of an engine. It was an SUV with black tinted windows, blocking my path.

The hairs along my arms stood up, signaling something was seriously wrong. A chill ran through me. I watched with disbelief and then horror as two shadowy figures jumped from the vehicle.

I didn't think. Spinning on my heel, I ran back toward the door, screaming at the top of my lungs. I felt the yank of my hair at the back of my head, slamming me against a hard body. I tried to scream again, but a hand cupped my mouth.

A familiar man's chilling voice uttered in my ear, "I told you the next time you let another man touch you, I would kill you both."

In that instant, I knew it was Carter.

My heart pounded, slamming against the walls of my chest with such intensity I was sure it would be my last breath.

The other shadowy figure snapped, "Carter, finish her."

Heat flushed through my body. "Fuck you. I'm not dying

without a fight," I ground out while throwing a hard elbow into his gut.

Carter slightly released his grip on me. I spun around, kneeing him dead in his nuts.

I cracked my knuckles before quickly getting into a warrior stance with my fists raised.

Carter's facial expression scrunched up with rage. His eyes turned crimson red, which was more animal than human—eyes just like the demon at Frank's house.

This confirmed my worst suspicion. Carter was a demon.

Carter's accomplice, a young man with mousy-brown hair and crimson-red eyes, ran toward me with an untamed growl.

The door slammed open, and Elijah emerged. He moved with lithe fluid motions, a catlike grace that seemed to fit him. His lips pulled back in a snarl. "It's time to die, demons."

Bam.

Elijah swooped forward with inhuman speed, punching Carter, sending him crashing against the building with a thud.

"Hope, move!" Elijah snapped as the mousy-haired man's clammy digits bit into my arm.

I swung around, punching the man in the face. "Elijah, I got —" I started to say but stopped short when Elijah roared so loud it made my bones shake.

Shreds of clothing scattered to the ground, revealing his heavily muscled nude body. I stared, slack-jawed, as Elijah's bone structure began to rearrange under his skin, expanding and stretching. Reddish-rusty fur grew, covering his entire body, and his feet and hands spread and thickened. A monstrous tiger stood in his place, his ears lying down flat, teeth bared, and eyes narrowed into thin slits, his tail hanging low.

I blinked rapidly, followed by an open stare.

Holy shit. Elijah's the tiger I've been dreaming about for months.

"Carter! Why didn't you tell me he's a fucking tiger-shifter?" the mousy-haired man yelled before he threw me to the ground.

The side of my head slammed against the hard surface.

Dazed, I watched the tiger, with one swift swipe of his gigantic claw, rip Carter's head from his body. Blood spewed from where his head used to be.

Carter's lifeless body lay before me.

The tiger roared, prowling toward the second man, who was begging for his life. Within seconds, the tiger leaped, biting into the man's throat, viciously yanking it out. Blood splattered the tiger's face as the man's body twitched and fell slowly to the ground. His bloody hands clenched where his throat once was.

There was a peaceful silence.

Carter and the man were dead. My life was mine again.

I sagged against the ground with relief. My eyes slid closed as I fought the dizziness from the dull thumping pain at the side of my head.

The tiger made a grunting noise. My eyelids cracked open to find the tiger looming over me. Its short muzzle opened, displaying a set of sharp teeth, but I wasn't afraid. He wouldn't hurt me.

This is Elijah.

When I extended my hand, the tiger tilted his large head down, rubbing against it with a rumbling of his throat and the blowing of warm air through its nostrils.

"Will you stop worrying? I'm okay. Just a little lightheaded." My digits caressed the blood-spattered white spot present on the back of its ear.

"I love you, too, putty cat," I whispered before slipping into the dark abyss of nothingness.

❧ 12 ❧

HOPE

THERE WAS A DULL, annoying pain in my head as I flipped over onto my stomach. I pressed my nose into the pillow, inhaling a lingering familiar aroma of earth, amber, and sandalwood, reminding me of Elijah.

Yummy.

Wait . . . what?

I jolted awake from lying tangled in the sheets on the king-size bed, sweating profusely. Scrambling to my knees, I tried to clear my sleep-fogged brain.

Where am I?

Easing back on my heels, I just sat there, blinking at the bright sunlight streaming across the massive foreign bedroom. The last thing I remembered was Elijah shifting into a tiger and killing Carter and his accomplice . . . who were demons.

"No." I frowned. "That can't be right. Demons and a tiger?"

The door swung open with Elijah standing in the threshold, looking refreshed and gorgeous. The man was huge, like an MMA fighter. My eyes boldly roamed up and down his body. His hardened abs rippled downward to his low-slung lounge pants.

Focus, Hope. Keep your eyes off his junk.

He ran a hand through his sleep-tousled hair. "Good morning, Hope," he drawled huskily, making no attempt to conceal the erection tenting the lightweight fabric of his pants.

"Was I delirious, or did you really shift into a tiger?" I croaked, clutching the sheet around me when I realized I was butt naked. I didn't want to think about the fact that he'd probably undressed me.

"Yep, that was me, your lovable putty cat." He chuckled.

My mouth dropped open and then closed. "Oh my fucking God, that wasn't a hallucination." It was a statement, not a question. "You're a shifter? What the hell is going on?"

"We have a lot to talk about, Hope."

"Yeah, you'd better start explaining, Tiger, because I'm about to get real rowdy." I scrambled off the bed, frantically looking around the room. "And where's my damn dress?"

"It was ruined by all the blood. Harper went over to your place and got some clothes. She left them over there." He pointed to the dressing table that had neatly folded garments stacked on top of it. "And that's my master bathroom." He pointed to the left.

"How long have you been a tiger-shifter?" I demanded.

He shrugged. "All my life."

"And what about Harper and Twitch? Are they tiger-shifters, too?"

"Nope. They're wolf-shifters," he finished.

"How didn't I know this?" I mumbled to myself, dissecting all my interactions with them in my head.

Not once had their behavior hinted of anything but human. My eyes widened when I started to recall all the little things that hadn't made sense, like Harper's vamps and sun comment. She was talking about real-life vampires. Then there was her strange request that I talk to Elijah about my encounter with the demon that had accosted Frank.

I'd just never connected the dots—until now.

"Hope, there was no way you could have figured out I was a shifter unless I revealed it."

"You did—last night at the dance-off." My lips pursed. "Your eyes morphed briefly, appearing more animal-like. Damn, I completely didn't put the pieces of the puzzle together. Holy shit!" I exclaimed. "Why didn't any of you tell me?"

I wasn't even going to dwell on the fact that my bestie was a shifter. That shit would be addressed when I choked her to death for not telling me.

He arched a brow. "Would you have believed us if we had?"

"Yes." I exhaled heavily. "Okay . . . that's a lie. Hell no, I wouldn't have believed you."

"Besides, shifters are forbidden to tell humans about our existence—well, correction, all Others. That includes vampires, shifters, and demons. All are prohibited from revealing their true nature—unless they're our mates. Still, disclosing our secret makes it . . . complicated. And the few humans who do know about us are sworn to secrecy." He pointedly stared at me.

I scoffed. "Why the hell are you staring at me like that? I can keep a fucking secret, Tiger. And even if I were crazy enough to go running through Manhattan, screaming that supernatural beings existed, who would believe me? I'd just end up in some padded cell, rocking back and forth." I bit my bottom lip. "All the guests at the charity event . . . were they Others, too?"

"Most of them. Very few in attendance were humans unless they were mates or consorts of Others."

I took a deep breath. "Mates, consorts, shifters, Others . . . I'm going to need a cheat sheet to figure all this shit out."

He pensively contemplated me. "So now that you know I'm a shifter, does it change anything between us?"

"I accept you for who and what you are. Granted, I have a ton of questions about shifters, but we have time for you to unravel that mystery for me." I paused when something else occurred to me. "Last night, you said you wanted to be with me."

"I still do . . . forever."

Now that Carter was out of the picture, there would be no dark cloud of doom hanging over our heads. My mind whirled as

I contemplated the possibility of building a life and family with Elijah.

But I still needed to know something. "If that's the case, when were you going to tell me you're a tiger-shifter?"

"Not until you accepted and trusted me. Trust is important in any relationship, Hope. And last night was the first time you actually opened up to me."

"I was trying to protect you," I answered.

"You're fiercely protective, one of the many things I love about you. It shows you care about me."

My heart raced. "I do . . . a lot."

"You wouldn't be my true mate if you didn't." He smiled.

"And there goes that word again—*mate*. Where the hell is my glossary of Others terms?"

He chuckled. "We have a lifetime together, darling. You'll learn quickly." He winked at me. "Meet me in the kitchen when you're done." He backed out of the room, closing the door behind him with a click.

My mind whirled with questions as I dropped the sheet. *What in the world is a mate? And exactly how many of my friends are Others?*

Snatching the bundle of clothes off the dressing table, I headed to the bathroom, closing the door behind me. The space was immaculate, with bottles perfectly lined up and towels stacked neatly. My toiletries were the only things out of place. Harper had brought over my bottles of body wash and lotion along with my toothbrush.

Turning on the shower, I adjusted the temperature before stepping beneath the rain showerhead. The jets beat against my body as I soaped myself up. I washed myself, rinsed away the soap, and stepped out of the shower. Snatching one of the luxurious towels, I dried myself off and brushed my teeth before putting on my lingerie. Pulling on a classic racer-back tank, I teamed it with a short denim skirt and a pair of front-zip lug-sole booties.

I stared at my face in the mirror. As usual, there were no signs on my face or body of being slammed to the ground last night. I had the freakish ability to recover from cuts and scrapes fairly quickly, and I never got sick.

"Good genetics," Frank had always said.

I shook off the sadness, remembering he was no longer with me. I had to be strong. I also had to call Cassidy and check in to see if he had any leads on Frank's murderer.

I pulled my hair into a high ponytail, leaving the bathroom. Stepping out of the bedroom and into a hallway, I followed it to a massive open-space concept living room with a kitchen on the left. Elijah was fully dressed with his hair slightly damp as he leaned against the granite counter.

He pushed a steaming cup of espresso across the counter within reach of my fingers. "How do you feel? Are you okay?" he asked.

Greedily grabbing the cup, I moaned with pleasure as the mellow blend rolled over my tongue. "Physically, I feel great, but mentally, I'm still reeling from everything, including the fact that Carter actually tried to kill me—again." I hopped on the stool.

"So you never knew he was a demon?" Elijah asked, walking around the granite counter. Grabbing the bottle of orange juice, he poured it into two glasses.

"Of course not. I knew he was deranged and suspected something was oddly animalistic about him, but I never knew demons were even real—until I saw one at my Uncle Frank's house yesterday."

His body tensed as he placed the bottle back onto the counter with a thump. "What did it want with him?"

"A deal gone bad. Frank said demons hired him to find an artifact, but he ended up stealing money from them." I gripped my cup with trembling fingers. "But I don't think he told me the whole story. He did that sometimes—you know, omitted the truth. Now I'll never know the real deal behind the demon's visit because he was killed in a drive-by shooting yesterday."

"I'm sorry." Elijah rubbed my hand. "Demons are shady. You can't trust them, and you most certainly don't ever want to cross them. But I suspect your uncle knew exactly what he was getting into when he decided to make a deal with them." He frowned. "Or he had to be real desperate."

There was heaviness in my chest and limbs when I thought about Frank. "Probably both. He was a good man who just made some really fucked-up decisions in life. But he didn't deserve to be killed for them." I blinked back the tears. "That's why I have to find out if and why they killed him." I pushed the coffee away.

He clasped my fingers. "I'll help you in any way I can. I'll call in a few favors and see where it leads."

All the tension in my body released as I squeezed his hand. "Thank you. I'm going to need all the help I can get. The only leads I have right now are something Frank told me to get from his safe deposit box if anything happened to him and my contact, NYPD Detective—"

"Shawn Cassidy." He interrupted.

"You know him?"

"Yes. I work with him from time to time on cases involving Others' attacks on humans." He picked up a glass and guzzled it.

I held up a hand. "Oh God, don't tell me. He's an Other?"

He shrugged. "Yes, he's a bear-shifter." He slammed his glass onto the counter.

I blinked. "Is there anyone I know who isn't an Other?"

He chuckled. "So far, it sure doesn't seem like it."

"So are you some sort of police officer?"

My tongue darted out to touch my lips. Just thinking about how hot he would look in a uniform while ordering me to bend over the hood of his car and giving me the hottest search ever made my clit thump.

His lips curled up into a small smile, as if he knew about my naughty, dirty thoughts. "No. Twitch and I work for a paranormal agency called Rogue. I'm a Hunter. I'm assigned missions to track down dangerous Others that have killed Others or humans. My job is to bring them in for justice, one way or another."

"One way or another? What's that supposed to mean?"

"Well . . . as a top Hunter, I always find my target, but most of the time, they're better off if I put them out of their misery, especially the ones that can't be rehabilitated," he stated dryly. "Dealing with Others is sometimes ugly but very necessary business."

This was a side of Elijah I'd never seen before. It was wild, dangerous, and sexy as all hell.

I beckoned him over with a finger. "Come here."

He stepped around the counter, caging me, making sure my body was flush against his.

I grabbed his face between my hands and stared at him. "Show me your tiger."

My pulse raced with excitement as his eyes transformed from amber to glowing golden feline slits. My eyes widened when I felt the slide of his tiger underneath my fingers. Elijah tilted his head down, rubbing it against my hands. His eyes closed. Using one hand, I dragged my fingers through his hair, and Elijah chuffed in response, a low sound that seemed to come from deep down in his gut. It was amazing how close his beast was to the surface.

"Don't ask me how or even why I know this, but your tiger seems . . ." I searched for the right word. "Agitated. Am I doing something wrong?" I snatched my hands away.

"Quite the contrary." His voice was low and husky. "He's so riled up by your delicious scent that he wants out so he can scent-mark my whole damn penthouse."

I laughed. "He's a possessive little thing."

Grabbing his face, my fingers tingled strangely. His beast pressed forward. Something stirred within me.

He took a breath. "I wouldn't bring out the tiger right now."

"Quiet, Tiger," I answered.

Going on pure instinct, I glided my fingers across his jaw. A soft pulse of energy whipped through my body, and the beast fell back.

Elijah's eyes transformed back to human. "What did you do? Now he's rolled over onto his back, limbs up and chuffing like a lunatic."

I shrugged. "I don't know."

He arched a brow. "Are you ready to tell me what you are?"

I frowned. "What kind of damn question is that? Human. African-American. Female."

"There is no way you're human. You took a lot of bumps and bruises last night, but I don't see any signs of it. That's not normal."

"It's no big deal." I shrugged. "I've been like that all my life. My uncle always said I was special."

"You are special to me." He caressed my face. "But I can sense there's something different about you. I just can't put my finger on it." He paused. "And I know of every race of Others on this planet."

I cupped his face. "I've never seen this side of you. You're frustrated because you don't have the answer." I bit his lower lip before softly kissing him. "It's kind of hot."

He flinched in pain.

"What's wrong?" I asked.

"My tiger is fighting to come out. He wants to mate and claim you."

"Mate? What does that mean?"

"When a shifter finds his mate, it's like finding a lost piece of himself. He feels complete, whole."

I swallowed hard. "Soul mates. That's what my dreams meant," I whispered, gazing into his eyes. "I've had weird dreams with you in them since the day I met you."

He blinked in confusion. "Interesting."

I bounced my foot. "This is going to sound insane."

He arched a brow. "Crazier than a man who can shift into a tiger? I doubt it."

"God, I guess you're right." I brushed my chest against his. "Each dream had me sitting on a rock, butt naked, while eye-stalking a tiger."

His lips curled into a smile. "This is sounding better and better . . ."

I laughed, slapping his arm. "Stop it. It's embarrassing enough, revealing my kinky dreams about you."

His face sobered. "Go on, darling." He cupped my cheek. "No judgment here."

"Every dream, I would just walk across the clearing and sit on a rock, just staring at a tiger standing in a river. The tiger would come over and greet me, and then the dream would be over." I bit my bottom lip. "But my last dream . . . well, it was different. As usual, the tiger came out of the river and greeted me." I reached up, running my fingers through his hair. "But here's the new part . . . This deer came out of nowhere, and you killed it, offering it to me. And then the tiger transformed into you." I paused. "How did I dream that before I even knew you were a shifter?"

He frowned. "I've never heard of a human having that ability."

"Is that bad?"

He shook his head. "No. Just unusual for a human."

I breathed out with relief. "Elijah, what I'm trying to say is you're not the only one who feels something. All this time was wasted while I was trying to deny my feelings for you because I was stubborn and, frankly, scared to fucking death to acknowledge them when all the signs in the universe were pointing to you. Please forgive me for all the cruel things I said last night. It was stupid to push you away. And if you still want to give us a try, I'll do everything in my power to make us work." I swallowed hard, feeling the swell of emotions rise within me. "Because I can't imagine a life that doesn't have you in it."

"Neither can I. Hope Pippa, you are mine, now and forever," he assured me before his mouth crushed mine.

His tongue thrust forcefully between my lips, sweeping against mine. My tongue slid around the tip of his and then rubbed under it. I couldn't get enough of him. I was grinding against him until he hoisted me up, curving my legs around his hips. Helplessly, I moaned with pleasure into his mouth, digging my nails into his back.

I nearly swallowed my tongue when he lifted me, yanking my skirt up, before setting me on the countertop. He gently pushed me back, one hand firmly grabbing ahold of my wrists, while his legs forced my knees apart. His free hand ripped my panties off and slid into my pussy, two fingers pushing inside, stretching me open. I moaned as I clenched those fingers tight. He growled.

His hand slid to my right hip with his fingers tracing slowly against my skin. "How long have you had this upside-down triangle mark on your hip?" he demanded.

"For as long as I can remember," I replied. "Why?"

Arching down, he rubbed his nose against my neck. "We have to go to your uncle's safe deposit box. It might confirm my suspicion about what you are."

"Now?" I inquired. "We're in the middle of something here, Tiger. And I haven't been fucked in years."

His head snapped up, giving me an honest-to-goodness bad-boy smile. "Good to know." He offered me his hand, pulling me off the countertop. "When we get back from the bank, I'll make sure to do a bang-up job when I take you all over my penthouse." He kissed me hard on the lips before stepping back. "Now let's get out of here."

13

HOPE

ELIJAH and I walked up to the receptionist.

"I'm here about an account," I stated.

The receptionist nodded and pulled out a pen and bank slip. "Please write your account number here. I'll direct you to the appropriate officer."

Taking the pen, I wrote the number Frank had given me.

Within minutes, a well-dressed man approached. "Come with me," he requested.

I followed him with Elijah clutching my now sweaty hand. We stopped in front of the bank's security checkpoint.

My eyes widened at the ultra tech device manned by two serious bank guards.

Elijah arched down. "It's a biometric scanner," he informed against my ear.

There was something ominous about coming to this bank.

What if I'm not human? What if my whole life has been one big lie?

The officer cleared his throat. "Ms. Pippa, they're waiting for your hand."

I blinked, focusing. *Here we go.*

Guiding my open palm onto the mirrored scanning surface, I

caught my reflection for a moment before a wave of white light passed beneath my hand.

The two guards stepped aside, allowing us entry past the checkpoint and into the bank hallway. A third guard led us to a special elevator. It took only moments for the elevator doors to open, and we stepped in and were sealed inside. It was a short ride before the doors opened again.

Stepping out, we found a man waiting.

"Mr. Reilly." An anal-looking man introduced himself. "Ms. Pippa, I assume you're here about your box."

"Yes," I replied.

Reilly nodded and gestured down the corridor.

We traveled toward the direction Reilly had indicated.

"This is unreal. I feel like Alice in Wonderland," I whispered to Elijah, surveying the sterile and kind of odd bank safe deposit viewing room with total privacy.

I sat down with Elijah standing next to me for moral support.

The deposit guard placed a large safe deposit box before me and then exited the room, closing the door behind him.

Elijah and I were alone.

Glancing up at him, I asked, "How did that scanning thing work? I've never been here before."

"This bank and several others are owned by a family of Nephilim—hybrids born from the union of an angel and a human. They must have received your DNA from your parents and programmed it into the scanner."

"Wow." I blinked. "This whole Others thing keeps getting weirder and weirder." And I hadn't even opened the box right in front of me.

This is it—the answers.

I lifted the lid to the box. There was a shallow tray on top. In the tray was a silver necklace with a large pendant and two envelopes. Mesmerized, I ran my finger across the sparkling bright blood-red stones, and a zing of energy coursed through it. Quickly, I pulled my hand away.

"That's odd," I murmured while pulling out the two envelopes.

"I'm going to give you some space to read the contents in private," Elijah announced before moving away.

"Don't you dare, Tiger." I grabbed his hand. "You're with me for better or for worse."

He stroked his thumb over my hand. "I wouldn't have it any other way." He raised my digits to his lips, kissing them one by one before releasing me.

I stared at the first envelope for what seemed like eons before my trembling fingers broke the red wax seal. I pulled out the letter and read the contents aloud.

~

"My sweet Hope,

"There are so many things I've longed to tell you and show you, but sadly, I've run out of time. So I leave this letter as a last resort.

"You are the only remaining full-blooded fae on the human realm. You have the ability to control all elements—fire, air, water, and earth. And you will come into your powers starting on your twenty-fifth birthday.

"This gift is a blessing and a curse. There will be Others that will seek to use you and Others that will offer to guide you on the right path. Understand their motivations before revealing your true nature.

"Lastly, the map I've left shows where the portals to the realms are located. Keep it safe, for it is the last of its kind.

~

"Love always,

Mom"

~

My posture slumped slightly. *I am a fae?*

Everything that I had known to be true was slowly crumbling around me.

Cautiously, I pulled the necklace from the box, warily watching as it swayed back and forth from my fingers.

Elijah gently took the necklace from me, unhooked it, and lovingly placed it around my neck. With fascination, I inspected the strange scarlet pendant that lay against my chest. My eyes narrowed on the intricate design of the silver circle encrusted with five rubies—a huge ruby in the center and four smaller ones encircling it.

"What are these strange symbols under the rubies?" I asked.

"Fire, air, water, and earth. And the one in the middle is spirit," Elijah informed gruffly.

"I guess you were right. I'm not human. What the hell is a fae?"

He rubbed his brow. "An Other that has the ability to control the elements—fire, air, water, and earth. No wonder I didn't know what type of Other you were. You are the last of the full-blooded fae on this realm. Let me see the other document from the box."

After handing it to him, he opened the envelope, carefully pulling out the folded paper. Unfolding it, he spread it out onto the table. Like my mother's letter confessed, it was a map.

"Fuck." He pounded on the table. "It's real."

"What's wrong?"

"I thought that the existence of this map was all legend. Elder Others have been talking about it for centuries. It's a map that has the locations of portals to different realms."

"I don't get the problem, Elijah."

"If you think demons are dangerous, imagine Others that are five times as ruthless and are waiting for someone to open their portal, giving them access to the human realm. It could start the apocalypse."

"Oh God, like end-of-days apocalypse?" My mouth slackened.

He nodded with his lips flattened.

Feeling overheated, I asked, "Why would she leave something so crucial to man's survival with me?" My mind raced, searching for answers. This whole thing didn't make sense.

"Who else would she have trusted to guard the map from getting into evil hands?" Elijah asked.

"I can't save the fucking world, Elijah. I don't even know anything about being a fae." I was trying to slow down my pulse, feeling myself sliding into a tailspin of panic. I couldn't protect the map or the world. Besides, I didn't want that responsibility.

Examining the map closely, I noticed it didn't even have any X-marks-the-spot symbols. "But this map doesn't have any specific locations noted for the portals. There's no way to find them."

"Your mother wouldn't have left you a useless map." His hands clenched and unclenched. "I need to brief Rogue and my team about this. We also need to find someone who can explain what to expect when it comes to your powers." His jaw tightened. "This changes everything, Hope. And the man you called Uncle Frank, I suspect he was your guardian. He probably was a demon."

I shook my head. "Impossible. Don't you think I would have known if he was a demon?"

His brows furrowed. "How? Up until yesterday, you had no idea Others existed." He paused. "There isn't a whole lot of information on fae because they are very secretive. But what I do know from reading the Others' historical archives is, for centuries, all full-blooded fae were assigned guardians. In essence, guardians would swear with their lives to protect their charge—their appointed fae. Your parents probably assigned Frank as your guardian before they died."

My pulse was racing as I tried to sort out this mess without freaking the fuck out. "Why is this all happening now?" I asked with a pain-filled voice.

He pulled me up, tenderly wrapping his arms around me. "Maybe Frank inadvertently revealed your existence to demons. Now, the demons probably want to possess the key to open the portal to the demon world. If their portal is reopened, the demons will have free rein to come to our world, and they will annihilate not only humans, but also Others."

I gasped. "*I'm* the key." Now everything started to come into focus. "Shit. Frank told me the demons gave him money to find the key. All this time, he was hiding the key in plain sight . . . me."

"Yes, Hope. With the map, your potential powers, and the pendant, that makes you one powerful woman."

"Do you think the demons killed Frank?" My mouth tightened.

"I wouldn't put it past them. But right now, we have bigger issues. If the demons know you're the key, they won't stop until they have you."

"I feel like I have some damn black cloud hanging over my head. First, it was Carter, and now, it's the demons." I swallowed hard. "I wouldn't blame you if you hightailed it away from me and this mess."

He grabbed my face between his hands. "There are no such things as coincidences in the Others world. I've known from the moment I met you that you are different. I felt a pull . . . a need to stay by your side. My tiger knew what you were, but I was stubborn. I'd been alone for so long that I grew to tolerate it, always telling myself that finding a true mate wasn't possible for a tiger-shifter, that we were loners. But there you were . . . a gift that had come into my life without warning, giving me hope that you would someday become mine to love for eternity."

Damn, this man was determined to bring me to happy tears.

"My whole life, I'd searched for that one person I knew would love me forever, someone who would be there for me when I needed him, someone who would keep me safe, a man I could act like myself with and have no worries that I'd somehow chase him away if I revealed my inner demons. Never in my wildest dreams had I thought I'd have the real thing—a man who, when I looked into his eyes, I could see the passion and fire I'd been praying to find. Thank you for not giving up on me and on us."

"You are mine, and I am forever yours, Hope. I'd move mountains to remain by your side." He arched down and kissed me hard and deep. He broke off the exchange and growled, "Now let's find out what we can do to stop the demons."

❧ 14 ❧

HOPE

I HAD a series of calls to make after Elijah whisked me out of the bank.

I chewed out Harper for not telling me she was a wolf-shifter, but that part of the conversation paled in comparison to the real important developments—like Carter and Frank now being dead and my newly discovered fae status and everything that came with it, including crazy demons.

Elijah called his team and contacts to dig up all the information he could on demons and to locate someone who had credible insights into the fae culture and powers.

We also stopped at my townhouse for me to pick up some clothes. I'd made sure to pack mostly casual and workout outfits and footwear that didn't require much fuss but were sexy.

It didn't take long for us to settle into a comfortable silence as we sat in his low-slung car and headed to the Rogue satellite office located in some secret location in Manhattan. The only knowledge I had of his presence was the one hand firmly gripping my thigh while the other clutched the steering wheel.

Intermittently, I'd pepper him with questions I had whirling in my head about fae, like what it meant to have the ability to control elements and where the fae had gone if I was indeed the last of my kind. But I quickly realized he really didn't know much about the fae that wasn't steeped in folklore, legends, and hearsay. The fae were a black box that no one had seemed to crack, and that didn't leave me feeling warm and fuzzy about the mystery shrouding them.

I would be screwed if I couldn't find a fae mentor to help me learn about my powers and give me information on what to do to prevent the demons from coming after me.

However, Elijah was well versed on all Others cultures besides fae, and he filled in the gaps I had about vampires and shifters. He blew my mind when he told me there were many types of shifters besides tigers, wolves, and bears—like lions, panthers, hyenas, foxes, rabbits, dragons, and cheetahs, to name a few.

"So explain to me what this whole mate thing is actually about," I prompted.

"What do you want to know?"

"Is there some crazy tiger ritual we have to do?"

He squeezed my thigh. "I'll have to claim and mark you at some point."

"Mark?" I scrunched up my nose. "Oh, for fuck's sake. Please don't tell me this shit has anything to do with urinating on me, because I'm so not down with that."

He replied, "Not," as he chuckled. "It's a bite that goes on your shoulder. It lets Others know you and I are mated for life and we are one. It also warns them there will be hell to pay if they fuck with you."

"In other words, you'll rip their damn throats out."

"To say the least," he growled. "And there is my mother. You'll have to be prepared for that tornado when I bring you to meet her."

Uh-oh . . . Please, no mother drama. "Why? You don't think she'll like me?"

"No. She'll love you." He briefly grinned at me before turning back to pay attention to the road. "I told her about you, and she can't wait to meet you."

"So you told your mom about me. I hope I live up to the expectations." I turned my head to hide my smile.

"You already have, Hope."

I spun to stare at him. "That right there gave you bonus points, Tiger."

He waggled his eyebrows. "I'll be collecting that shit later . . . when I get you naked."

"What about your father? Are your parents divorced?"

His jaw tightened. "My father left after I was conceived. We don't have much of a relationship, and I'm perfectly fine with that. In fact, I prefer it."

I rubbed his hand. "I'm sorry if I brought up a touchy subject. It's just that, growing up without parents, I kind of envied people who had them. Frank tried his best to fill in where he could as a father, but I always wondered . . . what my life would have been like if they hadn't died." I also missed that mother's touch and female perspective, especially when I'd hit puberty, which was a really rough time for me.

"I'm a big disappointment to my father," he uttered. "For that matter, all of us are," he finished stiffly.

"Who's us?"

"I have three brothers, and we've firmly rejected the tiger-shifter old-school thought of mating. Tigers are inclined to be loners and tend to go their own ways, except when they wish to mate with each other."

"Hold the hell up. I thought *mate* was the equivalent of a *soul mate*?"

"There's a big difference between the two concepts. Finding your true mate is the connection that transcends sex. It's a match that completes you on both a physical and emotional level. Tiger-mating is just straight-up fucking, grunting, and trying to preserve the bloodline. After mating with my mother, my father left her, so she had to raise her cubs—

my three brothers and me—alone. As far as my father was concerned, we should be doing our tiger duty by spreading our seeds far and wide to ensure the continuation of my family's bloodline."

His hand tightened on the steering wheel. "That's not what I'm about, and neither are my brothers. I always knew if I ever found my mate, I'd stay by her side forever. And if she wanted cubs, it would be me and her raising them together." He paused. "I'm not going to pressure you, Hope, but I can't lie. After I've mated and claimed you and we've spent some time together, making our relationship strong, I wouldn't mind having children with you. But that's totally up to you."

He solemnly examined me. "Cubs or no cubs, I still want you."

My heart raced with excitement. He wanted a family . . . with me.

"You've just melted this hardcore Brooklyn girl's heart."

This was Elijah, raw and unadulterated, and I loved every bit of him.

"And to answer your question, I've always wanted a big family with lots of kids. So, yes, down the line, I would love to have your cubs . . . lots of them."

He smiled. "Damn, I've got myself a keeper."

I pressed my hand against his cheek. "And don't you forget it."

He turned his lips into my palm and quickly kissed it.

"I do have one more question about this mating thing," I countered.

"Anything," he grunted.

"Will it hurt?"

"What do you mean?"

"When you bite me?" I inquired.

Elijah burst out with laughter. "Only a little bit. And after we've gotten things sorted out with finding you a fae contact and getting rid of the demon problem, my mother will drive you insane with planning our mating ceremony—the equivalent to a wedding."

I rested my head against the soft leather headrest and closed my eyes, trying to imagine what it would be like to meet his mother and brothers.

Family. I will actually have a damn family.

The thought excited me and filled me with fear.

Will they even like me?

I was a fae that didn't know shit about my bloodline or powers.

I didn't know much about the shifter world, but I was pretty sure being a fae and clueless about my ancestry wasn't a good combination.

But I didn't give a shit. Elijah was mine, and I'd be damned if I let anyone chase me away. I was done with running. I'd already wasted too much time avoiding Elijah. I was staying, and we'd work through any obstacles . . . together.

I hadn't even realized I'd dozed off until Elijah's voice boomed, "We're here, Hope."

My eyes snapped open, and I watched him drive up to a huge gate in front of a nondescript building before pressing his thumb against a keypad. The gate slid open, allowing Elijah to quickly drive through, and then it closed smoothly behind us. He sped into an underground parking garage and turned the car off before stroking a finger along my cheek.

"Are you okay?" he asked.

"As okay as I can be after learning I'm the last full-blooded fae on the planet. Essentially, I'm the equivalent of a unicorn to Others." I hadn't figured out the upside to my dilemma.

"You'll adjust, given time. Just be patient with yourself." He nuzzled his face in my hair and then backed away. "It's time to meet my team of Hunters. Ready?"

I nodded. "Yes."

He caressed my cheek before sliding out of the car and

swiftly coming around to open my door. Elijah whisked me away from the car and into the building.

A man with chocolate-brown hair was standing in the lobby, waiting. He loudly sniffed the air while maintaining eye contact with Elijah, as if waiting for him to give him permission to talk.

I frowned. This must be some sort of shifter hierarchy protocol.

Elijah nodded, and the man turned to me with an easy smile.

"Nice to meet you, Hope Pippa," he greeted with a Southern drawl. "My name's Kraven."

Kraven's stature was intimidating. His entire body was one sheet of rippling muscles, and he had to be at least six three. But there was something about his demeanor that quickly put me at ease.

"Hi, Kraven. Nice to meet you," I answered.

Elijah ushered me toward the waiting elevator while asking, "Is everything ready upstairs?"

Kraven's smile disappeared. He cleared his throat. "Yes . . . but there's a problem."

"What problem?" Elijah snapped as we entered the elevator.

Kraven uncomfortably looked at me and then back at Elijah. "We picked up chatter on the Others network that the Shadows are plotting to kidnap Hope."

"Over my dead body." Elijah scowled. "And how the fuck did they find out about Hope so fast?"

"We're trying to figure that out," Kraven admitted.

"Who are the Shadows?" I asked once the doors closed.

"Fae groupies," Kraven answered.

"Basically, a clan of fanatic warlocks who worship the ground fae walk on," Elijah snarled.

The elevator opened. Elijah placed a hand on the small of my back, guiding me into the sleek office space that occupied one floor of a mammoth office building. The sitting area had leather couches and an elaborate coffee table with art books piled on top. A large flat-screen TV on one wall was tuned silently to the news channel.

Elijah continued. "The Shadows have done some really crazy things to show their devotion to the fae, even offering their wives to them in hopes the fae would breed with them. But, thank goodness, the fae refused. Shit went to hell when the fae disappeared off this planet. That's when the Shadows started stalking the Credences, a family of fae-witch hybrids. We heard the Shadows are obsessed with breeding with the Credence family to create a new race of fae."

"Credence?" I stopped in my tracks. "As in Knox Gunner's girlfriend, Storm Credence?"

Elijah eyed me. "Yes. And his brother, Ryker Alfero, mated Lightning Credence. She's Storm's cousin. The Shadows recently kidnapped Light. Now the whole Credence family is on high alert."

Holy shit. I'm in fucking trouble.

"If the Credence family are hybrids and I'm a full-blooded fae, that can't be good for me."

Damn. My situation was getting worse by the minute.

"It doesn't mean shit." Elijah wrapped a beefy arm around my waist, anchoring me to his side. "I'll fucking hunt and kill anyone who tries to take you away from me, wiping them out of existence."

The image of a commando Elijah going assassin crazy on Shadows and demons flitted through my head.

Shit is definitely about to hit the fan.

❦   15   ❦

ELIJAH

I WAS PISSED. *Why the fuck didn't Frank tell Hope the truth about her fae bloodline?*

To make matters worse, according to Hope, he'd made a deal with demons. They were notoriously deceitful. It wouldn't be easy for me to kill them all off because they either wandered in groups or armies.

Shit, this is bad.

I didn't even want to think about how I was going to contain the Shadows situation. I'd already had Twitch contact Ryker to get all the information he had about the Shadows. I also made a mental note to meet up with Ryker later this week to talk privately about our now mutual interest—destroying the Shadows—and to offer him my skills and resources to help him get his mate, Light Credence, back. After all, we had the same enemy, and working together to annihilate them would make everyone's life a hell of a lot more peaceful, especially mine, since I'd be able to keep Hope safe.

I entered the soundproof massive conference room with Hope holding my hand and Kraven trailing behind. I stepped over the threshold and nodded at Kraven, who shut the door.

Twitch and Cesar, members of my elite Rogue team, immediately stopped talking and stared at Hope.

"Hope, meet my team of Hunters. You already know Twitch. His expertise is hand-to-hand combat."

Her eyes widened. "Well . . . that's good to know."

"Hey, baby girl," Twitch greeted. "You're in excellent hands. Between that brute of a tiger and us, we'll protect you."

I pointed over at Cesar, who was slumped over his laptop. "That's Cesar. He's a wolf-shifter, an explosives expert, and a general badass."

Cesar smiled and waved.

I pointed over to Kraven. "You already met him. He's our weapons expert and a bear-shifter. He also tends to be a grumpy SOB."

"What the hell, bro?" Kraven protested. "Don't tell her that. You know I'm nothing but a cuddly polar bear."

I snorted. "Yeah, right." I pulled out a chair for Hope to take a seat. Once she was settled, I stared at my team. "Now—"

"Oh my God." Hope interrupted. "A polar bear?" She examined Kraven. "I don't care if this request sounds crazy as hell—because, frankly, it is—but I just have to see your bear."

Twitch burst out laughing. "Come on. Let her see your bear."

Cesar shook his head. "This is like an Animal Planet reality show, and I want no part of it." He flicked his finger on his laptop and pointed out something to Twitch.

"Is it rude to ask you to shift?" Hope asked.

"No." Kraven scratched his ear. "I don't have a problem shifting for you, but"—he glanced over at me and then back to Hope—"that will involve me getting stark naked."

She had an expression of intense thought on her face. "I'm not interested in your junk. Just the polar bear." Suddenly, she turned to me, grabbing my hand. "You don't mind, right?"

I shrugged. "Nope. Nudity isn't a big deal for shifters."

Plus, I wasn't concerned about Kraven's bear trying to attack or hurt Hope. Upon meeting Hope, Kraven's bear had sniffed her scent, which was mixed with mine. His animal had silently acknowledged she wasn't his mate.

She clapped her hands with excitement. "Okay, let's do this." She was practically bouncing up and down in her seat.

Twitch and Cesar were disinterested and were reviewing something on Cesar's laptop.

"All right," Kraven grunted, walking over to the far end of the room.

The conference room was gigantic, and there was a whole section empty.

Hope got up to follow him, and I grabbed her hand.

"Hold on there, darling. You're staying with me. I don't think his bear will hurt you, but it's better to err on the side of caution." I ushered her a good distance from Kraven and sat down, pulling her onto my lap.

Kraven quickly stripped. Stepping back, he let the shift take over. His skin rippled and his bones shifted and popped.

Hope gasped in awe as the monstrous polar bear appeared where Kraven had been standing just moments before. He licked his nose and then sniffed the air around him, throwing his head up to see what was near. He yawned loudly, and then he plopped his bear butt onto the ground and waited.

Hope stared at him for a few seconds, and then she glanced back over her shoulder at me. "I'll never get used to that," she mused before eyeballing Kraven. "Can I touch you?"

Kraven's ears twitched.

"He's cool with you touching him." I stood up, righting her onto her feet.

I slowly guided her forward, and she laughed as she reached out a hand toward Kraven's muzzle. He didn't move an inch. She looked so small compared to his body. Hope's fingers brushed his snout, and he nuzzled against her hand. Then he loudly blew out through his nose before sneezing.

Hope chuckled. "He's so soft. Thank you for indulging me, Kraven." She stepped back, turning around to face me. "And thank you, Tiger, for being so agreeable to my weird request." She kissed me hard on my lips before pulling back.

"Anything for you, darling," I replied huskily.

"Hey, guys," Cesar called out. "I've got the files from Ryker."

I pulled Hope back to the front of the table to sit down while Kraven shifted back to his human form and got dressed.

Leaning forward, I pressed my hands onto the table, allowing my power to roll off my body. "Twitch already filled you in on the fact that she's the last full-blooded fae and my mate. I've already briefed you that the legend of the portals is true. And Hope is the key to opening them. Needless to say, we have lots of work to do to prevent fucking chaos from breaking out when the news gets out to the Others." I took a cleansing breath before sitting down.

Kraven examined me with way-too-wise eyes. "We've got your back, Elijah. Whatever you need, we'll make it happen."

Cesar and Twitch nodded in agreement.

"Thank you," I remarked. "Let's review the intel so everyone's on the same damn page."

"Here's the information we received from Ryker." Cesar slid his finger across the laptop, and the myriad of monitors flicked to life.

My eyes narrowed on the streaming images from the crime scene, autopsy, and copies of the report appearing on the monitors. The photos depicted gruesome images of Others bodies with their hearts ripped out.

"All the Shadows handiwork, and they've also been buying up property in Manhattan," Cesar informed.

"We've also picked up unusual chatter in the Others network about humans purchasing Others' hearts," Twitch commented.

I shrugged. "Yes. But you and I know it's not as simple as taking our organs or blood and becoming a shifter or vampire. If that were the case, we would all be extinct by now. Once our organs leave our bodies, they die."

"Ryker says the Shadows have figured out how to bypass that," Twitch replied.

Kraven laughed. "Impossible."

"Not anymore," Cesar commented. "The Shadows know how to harvest Others' organs. It won't make the organ recipient an Other, but it will significantly extend their life. It's like the holy grail, the equivalent of a fountain of youth for humans."

I stared, dumbfounded. "They'll hunt Others like animals."

"They've already started," Twitch stated dryly. "Now the Shadows are everyone's problem." He pointedly stared at me.

"How is this tied to the demons?" I sat straight up.

I didn't like the sound of this at all. The few humans who knew of Others existence had been trying for centuries to get their hands on Others' organs. They believed, by implanting the organs into humans, they would somehow get Others' strengths and powers.

"The demons and Shadows are working together. The why . . . well, we couldn't make sense of." Twitch scrutinized Hope. "Until now. Hope can open the portals, allowing the demons to go back home, and she's also a full-blooded fae, exactly what the Shadows are after to breed a whole new race of fae."

A surveillance photo popped up on the monitor. It was of Declan, the leader of the top army of demons, and Baptiste Thomas, the leader of the Shadows, talking in some deserted parking lot.

The demons were fragmented between groups and armies with infighting for power. But Declan had carved out his own powerful empire in the Northeast. He was ruthless and had started out as a top contract killer. From time to time, he'd even do some contract work for Rogue. And if he was hooking up with the Shadows, it wasn't good news.

"That's the man!" Hope shouted, pointing to the monitor. "The blond guy."

"What man?" I replied.

"The demon I saw at Frank's house." She bit her bottom lip. "Who is he?"

My fists clenched and unclenched. "The leader of the most powerful army of demons in the Northeast."

The situation with the demons was worse than I'd originally thought. Picking off demons would be hard enough, but Declan would not be a piece of cake. I'd have to think of a whole new strategy now that I knew he was somehow involved with Frank.

"Damn," Cesar retorted. "This shit is getting deep."

Hope tensed. "Leader of demons? Okay, that doesn't sound good. Do you think he killed my uncle?"

"I don't know, but he's a top contract killer, so anything is possible," I answered.

"I won't be able to rest until I know for sure." Her mouth tightened.

"And we'll find out." I pushed a strand of her hair behind her ear. My cell rang. "Damn, it's Harpy." A catlike hiss escaped my mouth.

"What's a harpy?" Hope questioned me.

"My boss, Gina. When she's not around, we just call her Harpy because she's literally a harpy—a winged shifter with eight-inch talons that could rip into a person like butter."

"Wow, that's badass. I've got to meet her," Hope responded as if she were checking off a list of things to see and do.

I shook my head. "Believe me. You don't. Gina tends to have terrible mood swings."

The team had a habit of treading lightly around Gina. No one wanted to piss her off—well, unless someone had a death wish.

Cesar shuddered. "Not much frightens me, but there's something about Gina that's just not fucking civilized."

I answered my cell, listening to Gina's instructions. The more I heard, the more pissed off I became.

When the call ended, I stared at my team. "It's confirmed.

Not only does Declan's army know Hope's the key, but so does every demon group and army worth their salt."

Kraven groaned.

I continued. "The upside of this clusterfuck is Rogue has a demon in custody, and he's apparently going to be joining us on a little mission."

Hope sat up. "What mission?"

I pinched the bridge of my nose. "We have to find the portal to the fae world and pay the fae queen a visit. Harpy used a seer to talk to the queen across realms and briefed her about you. Apparently, she's expecting you." I glanced over at Twitch. "Go pick up the demon." I tapped out a text. "I just sent you the address where he's being held by our Hunters."

"Got it," Twitch replied. Walking out of the room, he muttered something under his breath about hating demons.

"Why is he joining us?" Hope asked, curious. "What aren't you telling me?"

"My men are smart enough to trust me and not ask questions I don't want to answer," I pointed out.

"In case you didn't notice, I'm not one of your men. I'm your mate, so answer the damn question before I punch you in the throat," Hope bit out.

My cock jumped with excitement from her threat of bodily harm. Even when she was violent, she made me want to fuck her in the worst way. I willed my cock to behave.

Clearing my throat, I answered, "The man they have in custody is a demon, and apparently, he's part fae. He's a member of a demon group that has been causing trouble lately in their battle with Declan for more territory, and he wants to get away from them. He knows you're the key to finding the portal entrance. He's agreed to give us all the information we need about the demons' plans to kidnap you in return for an opportunity for the fae queen to let him pass into her realm.

"It's still up to her, even if we get him to the portal, and we will make sure he's not followed. For some reason, my boss believes his story," I barked. "Cesar, you and Kraven need to recon the area where the portals are located to ensure no creepy-crawly scumbags are around."

Hope pulled out the map from her handbag, handing it to Cesar.

"On it!" Cesar shouted, scooping his laptop off the conference table.

He and Kraven disappeared out of the conference room.

"It's just you and me, Hope," I told her. "I need to teach you how to fight. We have a workout room down the hall. It's time to get down to business."

"Looking forward to it," Hope responded with a grin.

❧ 16 ❧

HOPE

I CHANGED into my workout wear that I'd packed when I'd made Elijah stop at my townhouse after we'd left the bank. He and I spent the next few hours sparring. After he'd flipped me onto the mat for the umpteenth time and I'd landed wrong with all the wind knocked from my lungs, I got real angry and started to give him a run for his money.

An hour later, a miracle happened, and I flipped him onto the mat.

"Yes." I danced around. "Big trees fall hard."

After a few moments, he sat up with his eyes boring into me. "Is the twerking really necessary?"

"Don't hate. It's my victory dance." I pumped my fist.

"You've taken defense lessons before?" he asked.

"Yes. After the whole Carter quagmire, I took a ton of self-defense classes. I even paid for personal training sessions with a professional MMA trainer." I grinned at him. "The trainer told me I was a natural."

"It's going to be real interesting to see how your powers amplify your fighting skills," Elijah muttered more to himself than to me. "I think I need a hot bath."

"A manly man, such as you, takes baths? Do you put bubbles

in there, too, Tiger?" I started laughing, offering him a hand to help him up.

Elijah gave me a once-over before sprinting nimbly to his feet. "Only if you join me," he joked. Then he kissed my temple. "I'm tired, and we're going to have a long day tomorrow. The fae portal is somewhere in the mountains. That means we're going to have to hike our way there." He wrapped an arm around my body, pulling me hard against his chest. "I think, though, I might have just enough energy to see how you do with riding my big surfboard in the bathtub."

My pulse raced with excitement. "Watch me ride that gigantic wave, baby."

Twitch barged into the workout room. "Hey, Elijah, the demon's here. What do you want me to do with him?"

"Keep him away from Hope," Elijah snarled as his arm protectively tightened around me.

I playfully shoved him. "Oh, cut the me-caveman shit. If your boss thought he was a real threat to us, I seriously doubt she'd have sent him here."

Twitch snorted, "True that."

Elijah shot him a glare that said, *Shut the fuck up.*

"Hope and I are going to bed. You keep doing what you're doing, but make sure Kraven and Cesar take turns in watching the demon. Keep me posted," he snapped. He escorted me out of the room and into one of the suites down the hall, where he slammed the door shut behind us.

"Are you angry or just anxious to get some alone time with me?" I joked. Then I saw the expression on his face. Something was bothering him. "Hey, Tiger, are you okay?"

"Yes, I'm fine," he told me, but the tension in his body and the strain on his face belied his words. "Shit. No, I'm not." He dragged his fingers through his hair. "Tomorrow's your damn birthday, and I've got no idea what's going to happen tonight. I don't know how it works. We didn't have any files on fae coming into their powers."

I kissed him hard on the mouth. "You worry too much."

I started removing my shirt when he knocked my hands away and hauled me over his shoulder in a fireman's carry.

"Forget the bath. I need my cock in you now," he grunted.

In a couple strides, he walked me through the living room and into the bedroom suite. Once he undressed me, he quickly stripped himself before hustling us into the shower.

"Come here," he ordered.

In one swift movement, he wrapped his arms around me, yanking me high against his chest. I gasped with pleasure as he braced me against the wall of the shower, burying his face into the crook of my neck, inhaling deeply. His head snapped up, and he watched me with emotions swirling around in the depths of his amber eyes.

"I love you, Hope," he declared gruffly. "And if anything happened to you . . . it would fucking break me."

His words broke the dam of emotions.

I wrapped my arms and legs around him. I ran my tongue along his jaw. "And I love you, Elijah." I swallowed hard. "My heart, my love, my body are yours to cherish, now and forever."

His lips curled up into the most beautiful smile I'd ever seen.

"As are mine, my beautiful fae. I love you and claim you as mine, my mate, forever." His voice broke.

Shaken, I clenched on to him, my body needy. Elijah tightened his hands on my butt, pulling me closer. His other hand possessively collared my throat, branding it as his. His eyes flashed gold, turning tiger, and then reverted back to amber.

"Exactly when did you know I was your mate?" I asked.

He stared into my eyes. "From the first day we met."

My breath hitched as I grabbed his face between my hands. "Why didn't you tell me?"

"You needed to come to me on your own. Love isn't something you can force." He placed my hand over his heart. "It comes naturally."

His mouth crushed mine, his tongue forcefully thrusting into my mouth. It was dominant, possessive, and accepting nothing less than my submission. He pulled back, soaped, and rinsed us off with quick, fluid movements. He effortlessly hauled me against his chest, cradling me, while carrying me out of the bathroom and placing me onto the king-size bed.

❧ 17 ❧

ELIJAH

MY FINGERS TANGLED in Hope's hair, and I pressed my head up against hers, our lips meshing into a hot, erotic kiss. My tongue slipped between her teeth. Moving my hands over her stomach, I touched her feminine curves. I loved how she felt against my body and hands.

Pressing kisses to her cheek, I slowly worked my mouth down. Her ebony skin was warm to the touch, and her skin smelled like lavender and vanilla soap and slightly of me.

I liked that she smelled like me. It made me want to rub my face all over her skin, marking her with my scent.

My tiger chuffed and sat down, seemingly placated that our mate was safe in my arms.

I worked my way lower, pressing a kiss against her belly button, until I settled between her legs. Kissing her inner thighs, I nibbled until she was moaning and spreading her legs wider. Slipping my hands under her ass, I squeezed her cheeks before burying my face against her flesh. Using my mouth, teeth, and lips, I searched all her folds and feminine warmth until I found the sensitive dark-purple nub beneath the soft curls she kept trimmed short.

She is simply fucking delicious.

Sucking her into my mouth, I used my tongue and lips to pleasure her until she was writhing on the bed, begging me not to stop. Her hips rotated up, grinding her body against my face harder. Her hands fisted in the bed sheets, and her head was thrown back with her eyes shut. I could see her stomach tightening and rippling as I worked her closer to an orgasm.

"Please, Elijah, don't stop," she told me, trapping my head with her thighs.

She was hot and ready, achy and needy. I could tell she wanted me, and just like that, I found the right motion with my tongue, sending her soaring over the edge into an explosive climax that had her biting her tongue to keep from screaming the walls down. She thrashed her head from side to side as her entire body convulsed on the bed.

I pressed gentle kisses to her thighs and then moved back up her body. "I'm ready to mate-claim my woman."

Reaching over into the nightstand, I opened the foil package and slipped a condom onto my hard, hot length. My engorged flesh sank between her sensitive folds, and my balls slapped against her passion-moistened depths. Her hips bucked.

With my fingers buried into the flesh at her hips, I held her still. "Slow, darling. I don't want to hurt you." I gave her wetness time to adjust to my girth.

Her body tensed again from my fullness in her tight passage. "Relax," I hissed.

She took a deep breath, and I tangled my hand into her hair, kissing her hard and then nibbling my way down her throat before resting on the juncture of her shoulder and neck. I scraped my teeth over the spot before biting down hard, breaking the skin. Hope moaned in ecstasy.

I sucked on the spot, leaving a distinctive mark—a mark letting all shifters know, without a doubt, she had been mate-claimed by none other than Elijah Beastie.

My head snapped up and my body tensed when I saw tears streaming down her face as her chest heaved.

"What's wrong?" I asked hurriedly.

Her hands trembled on my shoulders. "I'm fucking scared to death, Elijah. It's this weird feeling in the pit of my stomach that won't go away, like something bad is going to happen to me or you." She swallowed hard. "I'm strong, but I'm not strong enough to go through your death."

I kissed where I'd marked her, sending a shiver down her spine. "That's not going to happen. Please trust me on this. I belong to you." I brought her palm to rest on my chest over my thumping heart. "And you belong to me. No one takes what's mine."

"You're turning me into some emotional, crying chick."

"There's nothing weak about showing how much you want what we have, baby." I nipped her on her chin as I raised her leg, pulling it over my ass. "Now let me show you how much I need you." With one hard thrust, I drove into her, sending me to a place I could live forever . . . in pure ecstasy.

She shivered deliciously as I kissed her neck.

"Elijah," she gasped, digging her nails into my shoulders, as the orgasm gripped her.

I growled, "Mine." My nose pressed against her neck as I breathed in her scent.

When she fell asleep, I found myself having a hard time resting. Watching over her while she slept, I tucked a loose strand of her hair behind her ear and curled up around her, protecting her with my own body.

My mind wandered to all the possible complications that could occur on our hike tomorrow while trying to find the fae portal. Above all else, I was worried about keeping my mate safe and not being separated from her.

18

HOPE

I WOKE up the next morning, jerking awake. Sitting up, I eyed the spot on the bed next to me. Elijah was already gone. Rising, I grabbed a robe he'd left at the end of the bed for me, and then I proceeded into the bathroom to brush my teeth before going to search for my sexy mate.

I found him in the other room, glowering at the half-demon man who was also part fae. Neither of the men would budge, and both were intimidating forces.

Walking over to Elijah, I pressed a kiss to his cheek. "Good morning."

"Happy birthday," he told me, giving me a quick smile before going back to glaring at the demon.

Tilting my head, I watched the two of them have a little standoff with their gazes. "Are you going to eat him for breakfast, or is there some reason you're trying to kill the man with your eyes?" I asked him.

"Let's go get you dressed, and we'll talk. You need to eat, and then we need to start our hike to find the fae queen," Elijah told me. He grabbed my hand, ushering me out of the room.

I rolled my eyes. "What's the rush?" I argued.

"Don't be difficult, Hope," he grumbled.

We quickly took a shower together and dressed.

I was putting on my sneakers when my head snapped up to study him. "So I don't feel any different this morning," I informed him.

He turned around with a perplexed look on his face.

I continued. "I don't know what I expected. I guess fireworks? Lightning bolts shooting out of my ass? Maybe some kind of explosion in my head, letting me know who I am and what I can do?"

"According to the demon out there, your power comes over time once you reach your maturity—or at least, that's how it worked for him. I questioned him," Elijah admitted.

"Does that demon have a name?" I asked him as I finished tying my sneakers and stood up.

Walking over to Elijah, I hugged him. I knew he was worried, but he wouldn't admit it out loud—not without me bugging him for the truth.

"His name is Risk," Elijah gruffly told me.

I stared at him for a moment and then poked him. "Is there a problem with this . . . demon that makes you hate him so much?"

"I don't trust him. For that matter, I don't trust any demon."

There was a knock on the door, and then Cesar's voice came through from the other side.

"The recon is done. We're all clear of demons. The GPS coordinates are in, and we're set to go, Elijah, whenever you two are ready."

I reached out to open the door when he stopped me by placing his hand over mine.

"Hope, I just want to tell you something before we do this." Elijah's expression was serious.

"I'm listening," I assured, touching his cheek with my other hand.

"I love you, and I've waited my whole life for you. So don't do something crazy, like getting yourself killed, because I'll drag your beautiful ass back from the underworld and then slap that luscious butt until it's sore for disobeying me." Elijah opened the door, walking out and leaving me there to absorb his words.

Scurrying after him, I pinched his arm just hard enough to get his attention. "Ditto."

He kissed me hard on the lips. "Go eat, Hope. You'll need the energy."

"Okay, I'll be quick," I told him before swaying into the kitchen.

From the other room, I wasn't trying to eavesdrop, but I felt like I could feel and hear what Elijah and his team were saying. It was almost as if I were standing next to them. The buzzing in my head and ears got louder, and I finally slapped my hands over my ears to quiet it.

After a moment, the sounds and noises stopped, and I stood straighter again, only to turn and find Risk standing a few feet from me. He had a curious expression on his face, but he didn't come any closer.

"This is part of it, isn't it?" I asked him, realizing this wasn't something Elijah would be able to answer for me.

"Do you mean weird things that happen to all your senses? Yes, that's the start of it. Eventually, other things will manifest—powers, so to speak. I've had to carefully hide mine. I'm supposed to be a demon, not part fae." He gave me a half smile. "Elijah wouldn't let me near you, but I'm pleased to meet you, Hope. I'm really sorry about all this shit with the demons trying to kidnap you. I was born in the human realm, so their mission isn't mine."

"Is that why you agreed to help us?" I asked, buttering a piece of toast after it'd popped out of the toaster. Grabbing myself a glass of orange juice, I drank some and then ate my toast while I waited for Risk to talk to me.

"Yes, partially, and because I wanted out. If I'm not in this realm, they can't force me to keep doing things I don't agree with. The problem with demons is they travel in armies and groups. When they found me, I was hiding and morphing into my demon self. I didn't know what was wrong with me. I thought I was going insane. They saved my life and taught me how to be a demon. The problem was I'm not just a demon. I'm also part fae."

Risk got himself a glass and held it out to get some juice from the bottle I'd set on the counter. I poured him some and then nodded in understanding.

"I found out I was part of all this when I saw a demon holding my uncle against the wall with his bare hands. Let's just say it's been an interesting last few days, and I'll be glad to get some answers," I told him. I clinked my glass against his. "For luck. We might need it."

"That demon will need all the luck he can get if he keeps staring at you like that," Elijah growled from the doorway.

"Oh, knock it off, Tiger," I complained, giving Risk an apologetic glance. "I think he has major issues with demons," I said to Risk.

Risk shrugged. "Rightfully so. Demons are scary creatures to mess with, and they don't give up easily. If we can get to the portal safely before they realize you know where it is or where we've been, we'll stand a good chance of getting away. The problem will be what happens if we come back to this realm—if they'll still be here, waiting for us," Risk informed before finishing his juice and setting the cup on the counter. "They aren't stupid. They will figure out where we've gone, and they won't let go of their prey so simply."

"You let my team worry about that shit," Elijah snapped. "You just help Hope figure out how to open the portal when we get there. That's the only fucking reason you're even going."

I could tell Elijah didn't like a demon being so close to me, and it was making him act a little irrational.

Risk's eyes narrowed. "I've never opened a portal before. If I could, don't you think I'd have done it and sent the demons home to their realm? That's where they've wanted to go this whole time. That's why they want Hope so badly. They assume she can open a portal. Not every fae has the power to open it, and you're assuming she will already have that power by the time we get to the gate," Risk pointed out.

I realized Elijah, his team, and Harpy really didn't know enough about the fae to understand what we were getting ourselves into. We were all going into this shit blind.

Damn, this could go bad real fast.

I just hoped we survived this—at least long enough to get to the portal and to the fae queen.

❊ 19 ❊

ELIJAH

WE DROVE out to the woods, following the GPS. Hope and I were alone with Risk. Kraven, Twitch, and Cesar would go as far as the beginning of the woods, and then they'd stand guard until they got the signal that we were on the right track. Then they'd check in with Harpy and follow up with some other loose ends, like the Shadows and that fucking prick Declan.

It would be a long few miles' hike, and I wasn't looking forward to sharing my time with Hope with a demon. I knew Risk wasn't going to harm her, but that didn't mean I wanted his damn ass around either.

"I know this isn't your ideal date," Risk finally told me, giving me a quirky smile.

Good, Risk knows I hate him. That meant he would think twice before fucking around and getting on my damn nerves. My tiger was already roaring and scratching to rip into Risk's ass. Demons weren't exactly trustworthy, and I didn't believe his motives were entirely pure.

"Do you know how to access the portal even if you can't open it?" I asked him as I drove, my hands tight on the wheel.

Hope was in the backseat, safe, and Risk was in the front

127

passenger seat where I could keep an eye on him and toss his ass out if he even blinked at me wrong.

Risk shrugged. "Not exactly. I just know the fae are supposed to feel it. It's the kind of deal where we'll know it when we see it."

I drove the rest of the way in silence. My team trailed behind me, and when they got to the park, I tossed Twitch the keys to my car. "Go follow up on that intel we need. If my cell phone works, I'll call you, but I'm guessing cell reception doesn't work in the fae realm."

"I would imagine not since our resident Harpy has to use a seer to talk to the fae queen across realms." Twitch gave me a light cuff on the shoulder. "Safe travels, Elijah, and good luck. I wish I could go with you. I heard the fae women are freaks in the sheets."

"I'm not interested in fae women, just Hope," I reminded Twitch as I slapped him on the backside of the head. "Keep your thoughts to yourself, pervert."

"Whatever, bro," Twitch jeered before his face suddenly grew serious. "I mean it, Elijah. Bring her back safe, or Harper will have your ass for getting her bestie hurt."

"I will," I assured.

I said good-bye to my team, and then without a word to Risk, I clasped Hope's hand, and we started down the trail into the woods. According to our GPS and maps, it was a five-hour walk. If I could shift, I'd have been able to get there in two, but Hope wasn't a shifter, so I needed to stay in human form and go at her pace.

We walked for a couple hours before stopping to drink some water and take a ten-minute break. Hope seemed relaxed, but I was picking up on some serious tension from Risk.

"What's your problem?" I finally asked him. "You seem nervous."

"I was raised as a demon, I was born in the human world, and I have just enough fae blood in me to have powers and be able to pass through the portal. There's a good chance they might kill me on sight because of my demon blood," Risk pointed out as he rubbed his chin. "I don't know if this was a stupid idea, trying to get away from the demons by running to another supernatural group, or if it's the smartest thing I've ever done. I won't know until I've done it, and I can't take it back."

"Yeah, I can see why that would stress you out," I agreed, feeling a twinge of sympathy for the guy.

I didn't know his whole story, but I'd heard enough when I was briefed about why I had to take Risk with me, and I knew his life hadn't been easy.

❧ 20 ❧

HOPE

"LET'S KEEP MOVING!" I yelled.

I could feel the tension radiating off Risk, and it was making me antsy. I just wanted—no, I needed to keep moving.

We hiked for another few hours until we reached a spot that just felt . . . different to me. I could almost see a strange shimmer in the air, but it was unlike anything I'd ever seen before.

If I hadn't been looking for something out of place, I wasn't sure I would have even noticed it. It was almost like a ripple in the air that had a silver luster, barely detectable to the naked eye. When I walked over to it, I put my hand through it, and my digits disappeared.

"I think I've found it," I announced.

Whatever I had thought a portal would be in my head, it hadn't been this.

Taking Risk's hand into one of mine and Elijah's in the other, I walked through the ripple, tugging them with me. It felt like walking through a waterfall, except we were totally dry when we walked out on the other side.

But what I saw wasn't what I had expected, not at all. I'd anticipated armed guards. Instead, I'd landed in the middle of a freaky fae orgy. There were at least four people tangled in a sexual mess, with lots of moaning and nothing but bare asses, cocks, and breasts. Essentially, it was a sex circus.

I wasn't a prude, far from it, and some of the sexual positions I'd already stored in my memory bank for experimentation with my Elijah, but still, *what the hell?*

I glanced over at Elijah, whose face was all scrunched up, like he was witnessing a weird scientific experiment gone fucking wrong.

He shook his head. "Shifters are highly sexual and kinky as hell, but this right here . . . is all wrong." He blinked like he hoped the whole shit would disappear, or maybe he was just praying to be struck temporarily blind.

And then someone did a move that caught his interest because his head tilted and his eyes narrowed, as if he were taking notes.

I jabbed him hard in the side with my elbow. "Don't even think about it. We are not doing that position."

He focused on me with his lips curling up into a sexy smile. "But you're a dancer, so you can bend at that angle."

"Tiger, I'm not that fucking limber," I hissed. "Now look away before I gouge your fucking eyes out."

Jamming my hands on my hips, I just stared, dumbstruck, at the beautiful people with slightly pointed ears in the throes of passion, executing moves that were hotter and kinkier than any porn I'd seen.

"Hello?" I bellowed.

But the fae were completely oblivious to our presence.

"Where's the spray hose when you need it?" I grumbled.

"Well, this is some welcoming party," Risk muttered, his cheeks turning pink.

"Are you embarrassed, Demon?" Elijah laughed.

He rubbed his chin. "More like not expecting to be slammed in the face with a damn full-blown orgy," Risk replied indignantly.

Quickly finding the exit out of the room, Risk, Elijah, and I shut the door and landed in an ancient-looking brick hallway that reminded me of a castle from centuries ago, except it appeared to have modern conveniences. The lights weren't candles or fires; they were bright lights that lit up the halls.

"They have running water and electricity?" I asked Elijah, curious.

"Magic," Elijah quipped.

We wandered the halls until a man stopped us. He didn't seem surprised to see us, but he stared at Risk with an odd expression.

"We are here to see the fae queen. She's expecting us," Elijah told the man.

"This way, shifter," the man urged. Turning on his heel, he walked down the hallway.

Elijah and Risk easily kept pace with the fae, but I, on the other hand, nearly had to jog to keep up with him. When the man led us into a throne room, it was unlike anything I'd ever seen. Nearly everyone was naked and in some kind of sexual act.

"I love sex, but come on. This shit is ridiculous," I uttered. There was no way I could even imagine living in this sexual debauchery twenty-four-seven.

But it was the woman dancing in the center of the room who caught my attention. She was riveting as she shimmied before the man sitting in a chair, clearly aroused, indicated by his tented pants. The dancer's hips twisted, bumped, and circled in figure eights. She slid her head to the right and then the left while crossing her hands in front of her face. Then she spun around and started softly kicking her foot, like brushing sand off the floor. Her moves were big, full, and juicy.

My heart raced with excitement. "I'm definitely stealing those moves and adding them to my dance repertoire." I loved watching and learning from other dancers, which was why I made a point of partying occasionally at hip clubs whenever I traveled. It added that edgy flair to my choreography.

A beautiful woman with rich honey skin and thick, long curly hair that flowed past her shoulders was sitting in a throne-like chair, eating fruit that resembled a grape, watching the acts like it was her favorite reality show. Her dress was see-through and light pink, leaving nothing to the imagination.

Then the dancer did a killer move that made me want to jump up and down, clapping. She kicked her leg over the man's shoulder, and using her hand, she pulled her other leg over his shoulder, straddling him. Effortlessly, the man cradled her butt and then proceeded to nuzzle her inner thighs.

"I am the queen. And you must be Hope," the woman on the throne stated regally. She rose and practically glided toward us. Her curvy figure swayed, as if she understood all too well the power of her beauty and wasn't afraid to liberally wield it.

Her lips curled up into a welcoming smile as she placed her hand on Elijah's shoulder. "And you are Elijah, the tiger-shifter, her mate." She stared at him like a piece of steak she would love to eat.

Pointedly, I glared at her hand that seemed to take permanent residence on Elijah's bicep. "Don't even think about it. Hands off my mate," I gritted out. I didn't care if she were queen of the world. It was plain rude and disrespectful to poach another woman's lover.

The queen's violet-colored eyes sparkled with humor, but she immediately removed her hand. "Apologies," she stated with a graceful bow of her head.

"Sure you are," I remarked, giving her a once-over.

The queen lifted an eyebrow while staring at Risk. "And you are one tasty-looking specimen of—" Her mouth dropped open and her body stiffened. Then she cleared her throat. Raising her finger to beckon the man who had escorted us there, she whispered frantically to him.

Risk shifted from side to side before taking a step back, as if he were contemplating running out of the room. I could see a muscle in his jaw twitching from how stressed out he was about the situation.

"Is there a problem?" I asked.

Risk was a grown man who could handle his own business and safety, but it didn't seem right for me to stand idly by and not do or say shit.

"Not at all," the queen reassured coolly. "Quite the contrary."

"Sir," the man urged Risk, "if you'll please come with me, the queen would like a private audience with you."

"What?" Risk sputtered.

"It will be fine," the queen assured Risk while the man led him away.

"You don't plan on killing him, right?" Elijah asked, raising an eyebrow at the queen. "I wasn't particularly fond of the guy, but Gina might stab me with her talons if I didn't do shit to stop you from killing him."

"I have no intention of harming him." Her lips pursed before saying, "He's the spitting image of one of his ancestors. I thought that bloodline had been all but wiped from our lineage. It's pleasantly surprising." Her eyes narrowed. "He's at least half-demon though, isn't he? The potential there . . . ." Waving her hand, the queen abruptly changed subjects. "Never mind, you let me worry about him. Let's talk about why you are here."

❧ 21 ❧

HOPE

"Did you know my parents?" I asked the queen as Elijah and I sauntered beside her through the halls to a place where we could talk in private.

Everywhere we walked, I'd see two or more people involved in various forms of lovemaking or rough sex. I'd even seen one woman tied up and being spanked from behind while another man took her from the front. While the acts were wildly provocative, it wasn't something I was remotely interested in participating in. Now, if Harper were here, this would be her equivalent of nirvana.

"I don't know your father, but I grew up with your mother. What a wild thing she was." The queen's laughter was like a melodic tinkle. "All the stories I could tell you—"

"Please don't." I interrupted. I had no memories of my parents, and the last thing I wanted was a rehash of all the freaky shit my mother had done to be the only memories of her that stuck.

"Okay, got it." She winked at me. "Well, back to safer but less entertaining topics. Your mother left the fae world very young. She was always . . . How do you say? A romantic, and she believed her true mate was somewhere out there. I guess she proved me wrong. I just never believed she would find that special someone."

"Are you saying fae don't mate?" I asked.

"They do sometimes, but it's very rare. We, by nature, tend to be a naturally evolving species that don't like to limit ourselves to just one partner." She eyed the two of us with a raised brow. "You'll have to tell me what it's like to be mated."

"Check back with me in a couple months. I haven't been mated long enough to give you a fact-based opinion," I replied, waiting for the queen to shut the door.

She seemed to be relaxed about security, and it made me wonder how often they ever had to deal with the threat of violence.

I glanced at Elijah, who paced the perimeter of the room, as if checking to ensure the area was secure from intruders and danger.

The queen pointed over to the massive bookshelves that lined the walls from floor to ceiling. "I would offer you books on your lineage and how your powers will manifest over time, but I'm guessing no one has ever taught you how to read fae language. There are too many books for someone to sit here and read them to you, and based on your expression since you got here, you're not keen on staying in our realm," the queen added bluntly.

"You are correct. Do you have a first name?" I asked. I felt awkward addressing her by something as pretentious as Queen.

"You may call me Tianna."

"Tianna, I do appreciate you letting us come here, but this is not my world. Frankly, it would send me crazy, being around this ongoing sexual bonanza." I wrapped my arm around Elijah's waist. "Plus, he would never leave my side, and it would be unfair to expect Elijah to give up his life to be here. This realm wouldn't work for both of us."

"I understand and accept your decision. But I must warn you of the danger of being a fae in the human world. There are those who will seek to use your powers for evil, if they find out you are fae." Her face tightened. "We've had our share of crazies over the centuries, like a group of warlocks called the Shadows." She shook her head. "Bizarre people, those warlocks."

"What do you know about them?" Elijah asked.

"Centuries ago, both demons and warlocks were guardians to fae that ventured into the human world. The demon alliance worked well because they were strong warriors, but the warlocks, not so much. The warlocks did not have the fighting skills, but they were loyal to a fault. I'm not sure how and why the relationship between the fae and warlocks became unhealthy and toxic, because it was way before my time." She pursed her lips. "And, also, there's the fact that it was erased from the fae history books. But what I do know of them is not good. They are dark and dangerous." She stared at me. "This is why you must keep your true nature a well-guarded secret."

"Unfortunately, the demons and Shadows know of my existence," I countered.

"That is a sticky dilemma," Tianna responded.

Elijah growled, pinning me to his side. "I will hunt and kill every one of them before I let them near Hope."

"You just might have to, shifter," Tianna replied bluntly. "The Shadows are a depraved lot who are consumed with creating a race of fae in the human realm. Of course, I do have some things I can offer Hope for protection. And I have a seer who can enchant her necklace." She walked forward, touching the pendant.

"The enchantment will shield you from the Shadows and Others, like demons. They will not be able to detect anything about you but a human essence. Your necklace is powerful and can be used as a grounding stone to help you conceal and control any powers as they manifest. It will also give you a way to contact me, should you ever have the need or if you want to talk with our seer to ask questions about your powers and work on learning to control them."

It was a relief to know there would be someone to guide me through this whole fae transition.

"Do you have suggestions on how to get the demons off my back?" I asked.

"Yes, but I'm not sure you'll like it." Tianna rubbed my cheek with a perfect hand. "I think you should give them what they want but on your own terms, of course. They want to go home. They've been trying to find a way home for many, many years. If you have the power to open up a portal and send them home, offer to do that in return for leaving you alone. I'm guessing, if given an opportunity to go home, they'll take it."

"Bullshit," Elijah snapped. "They'll try to hurt Hope."

Damn. It never occurred to me to just offer the demons what they wanted.

"Hold on, Elijah." I squeezed his arm, studying Tianna for any hint of deception. "And if they try to force me to go with them?"

Elijah's fists clenched at his sides, and I swore I heard the grinding of his teeth.

The queen let out a loud laugh and shook her head. "Our energy opens the portal, allowing the demons access to pass through it. Demons cannot force a fae to go with them if we do not wish to. If a demon tries to pull us through with them, our power repels us from the portal's threshold. It's a safety mechanism."

Elijah scoffed, "Are you saying the fae, over the years, willingly went with them?"

"Do you really think demons and fae are all that different?" The queen arched a brow, regarding him. "At one point, we mingled freely. The demon wars put a stop to that because we chose not to get involved. Many fae have demon blood in their lines and vice versa. Demons are not our enemy. Though if they've been stuck in the human realm for a long time, they might have forgotten that."

I absorbed the news, and nothing seemed to make sense to

me when it came to the fae. "Is that why you allowed Risk entrance here?"

"No. I allowed Risk to come here because he's my mate."

My mouth dropped open, and then I closed it. "Excuse me? Did you just say mate?"

"He just doesn't know it yet," the queen replied, smiling. "Fae rarely mate, so when we find ours, we will do anything to keep them. A seer predicted him. I just didn't know when he'd land in my lap. I owe you a great debt for bringing him here, Hope. You can go or stay, but Risk must remain here."

I sputtered, pointing out the obvious, "You can't make him stay if he doesn't want to." I felt a chill go up my spine. I had a feeling Tianna was used to getting her way, even if she had the face of an angel. I knew stepping on her toes would be a bad idea, but I never backed down when I was right. "If he wants to stay, that's his fucking choice, not yours, Tianna."

"I never said I would force him, Hope, but leave it up to me, and I promise you he'll voluntarily stay." She paused. "As I said, the demons are not the enemies you think they are. Their time in your human world has warped them. The wars in the human world have changed them. They need to get back home if they are going to heal and find peace again. Demons are not monsters. They are just another race, like vampires or shifters."

Tianna tilted her head with her eyes narrowed. "Now, you must be tired from your journey. And I have a man to seduce. I will see you in the morning. Allow my servants to take you to your quarters so you can freshen up, and we will speak before you leave. I'll have my seer prepare the enchantment spell I promised. Oh, and, Elijah, tell your Harpy I have the item she requested. You can take it back to her."

Elijah nodded but was wise enough not to ask Tianna what it was.

Our escort came back into the room and waited patiently for us to follow him. With a small nudge at the small of my back, Elijah ushered me out. I tried to avoid watching all the fae having sex in the hallways and every corridor we passed as we were escorted along to a large set of double doors.

The man nodded and pushed the door open for us. The suite was large and decorated with ornate furniture. "There are two master bathrooms and clothing that you are welcome to slip into. Also, there are lots of condoms." He pointed to bowls placed strategically around the suite. "Do not hesitate to press the Service button"—he nodded to the panel on the wall—"if you require something that is not already provided within this suite. We tried to think of everything that would make your stay comfortable, but I'm sure we've missed some things. Once you press the Service button, a servant will promptly come to get you anything you need." He turned on his heel and quietly exited the suite.

When Elijah and I were finally alone together, I just stared at him. "I don't understand what just happened," I admitted.

Then I fell backward onto the bed and stared up at the ornate ceiling that had a large painting on it with water nymphs and mermaids coming out of the sea and clinging to rocks. It was intricate, and if I stared at it long enough, it appeared to be moving. "Tianna is quirky, to say the least. And that whole Risk thing sounded very *Silence of the Lambs*."

"I didn't realize fae were so fucking strange or that they had sex like damn rabbits." He sat on the bed next to me. "Well, at least you got the answers you wanted, but maybe not exactly how you wanted them. I don't know how I feel about you offering to help the demons, especially if they're behind the killing of your uncle. But if you do send them home, they obviously cannot fuck with you anymore," Elijah mused more to himself than to me.

"But the demons seem so prone to violence. I'm having a hard time, especially with the information Risk provided, thinking the demons can be reasoned with," I told him, rubbing my chin. "I don't even know how I'd offer to send them home if

I don't know how to pull up a portal, let alone control where it goes. None of this makes any sense to me."

"Yet." He leaned down, kissing me, before standing up and pulling out his cell. He paced from one end of the space to the next, holding his cell up in the air.

"Are you really trying to get reception? Here?" I rolled my eyes.

"It's not improbable," he grunted. "Shit." He raised it higher. "Yes, one bar—damn, it's gone." He shook his cell in the air as if willing it to work.

I rolled off the bed. "I'm going to take a shower. Tell me how the search for the elusive bar works out for you." I stepped into the bathroom, preparing to marvel at the splendor. I was not disappointed. It reminded me of a luxurious cave. All the walls were covered with jewel-like stones that glistened in the softly lit bathroom. Stripping off my clothes, I stepped into the glass enclosure, which sealed behind me.

"It must be motion activated," I remarked.

Seconds later, a plume of purple mist filled the enclosure, engulfing my naked body. I knew by the silkiness of the mist that it was body wash. The ceiling opened, trickling warm water all over my body, as I washed my downy mound, remembering the sensual touch of Elijah's hands all over me last night. When I was done washing off, I stood at the entrance, and the glass door opened, allowing me to exit.

Drying off quickly with a huge fluffy white towel that felt like silk against my skin, I leaned against the counter and examined my hair. It was now a huge mass of shiny thick curls that cascaded to my shoulders.

"Damn. There goes my carefully flat-ironed hair. Oh, well. Au naturel, it is." I sauntered into the walk-in closet, searching for something to wear.

An array of clothes hung from hangers on racks. The clothing was a rainbow of colors, and all of them were indecently see-through, reminding me of the outfit Tianna wore.

I pulled a gold-colored spaghetti-strap mini dress from a hanger and stared at it. "There is no way this thing is going to hold in all this ass and tits." Tugging it over my head, the material clung to my body, pulling in all the lumps and bumps like a girdle, minus the I-feel-like-a-sausage sensation.

"Damn, it's magic fabric." My breasts were held up like I was wearing a bra. Turning around, I gazed at my ass over my shoulder in the mirror. "Holy shit." The material hugged my ass so tight I swore it was lifted a little.

Note to self: Ask Tianna to get me a dozen of these outfits in every color imaginable.

I spun around, observing my body in every position possible. I looked sexy. Between the outfit and my mass of curls that were like a cloud of goodness, I was ready to tackle Elijah and ride his face like he was a stallion.

Popping open the bathroom door, the low strands of Middle Eastern music greeted me with a hip-hop edge floating through the air. Elijah was sprawled across the bed, rolled onto his back, both arms over his head and legs stretching out long. He was bare-chested and wearing lounge pants that were so sheer it allowed me to see his big golden thighs.

I posed in the doorway, like a vixen, with my back against the doorjamb and my hips circling in slow figure eights to the music as I waited for him to notice me.

His head snapped in my direction. "Damn, you look good enough to eat. I love your hair curly. It makes you look more exotic."

"I'll have you know I've put at least one of my hairstylists' kids through college with the amount of money I've spent on getting my hair flat-ironed."

He smiled. "Straight or curly, I don't give a shit. You're beautiful to me. Now get over here and sit that gorgeous pussy on my face."

"Nope." I twisted a curly strand of hair around my finger. "Not until I show you my freaky, naughty moves." I pointed to the chair in the far corner of the suite. "Bring that front and center and sit your sexy ass down. Let your mate show you how much she wants you."

Elijah's lips curled up into a bad-boy smile before he got up.

I licked my lips while gazing at his tight butt.

Damn, he has the hottest ass I've ever seen.

He dragged the chair by the bed, sitting down with his muscled legs wide. "Show me what you're working with, darling," he ordered with a gruff tone. He faced me, giving me a sexy and in-control stare.

I pushed away from the doorway with a bouncy strut. I was an exhibitionist by nature, and seducing him with a little strip-tease ramped up my adrenaline, making me giddy with lust. When I reached him, I unhurriedly circled his chair, giving him my best smoldering gaze while running my fingers against his neck. As I passed behind him, I leaned over, brushing my breasts against his back before running my tongue along his ear. "How much do you want it, baby?" I whispered before trailing my tongue across his neck.

He reached up and grabbed the back of my hair. He growled in the sexiest voice I'd ever heard, "So bad all I can think of is shoving my cock so far into your dripping pussy that all you can taste is me." He slowly released my hair.

I twirled around him, stopping in front of him. I bent over at the waist, practically putting my ass in his face. "Do you want to touch it, baby?" My breathing hitched as I felt his fingers run along my ass seam.

"You have the sexiest ass I've ever seen. I can't wait to take you from behind."

I tauntingly wiggled my ass.

He slapped my ass cheek so hard that I knew I would have a handprint. I moaned when the delicious zing traveled straight to my throbbing core. He rubbed his hand over the cheek, soothing the pain of the sting.

I spun around, walking over to him. "Did I displease you, Tiger?" I asked with a flirtatious smile.

"There's nothing your sexy body could do to displease me . . . besides disobey." He sternly looked at me.

"Will you punish me?" *Please say yes!*

"Strip," Elijah demanded with a strong voice.

I tugged off the spaghetti-strap dress. There was something so intimate and hot as I stared into his eyes while slowly peeling it off, letting it pool at my feet before kicking it away. Now I was completely nude. "Like this?"

He grinned, his teeth flashing white. "Fucking lickable. Now come to me."

Tweaking my nipples to make them erect, I walked languidly toward him and swung my foot up onto his shoulder.

"Shit," he groaned. "You're so wet." He swooped down, sliding his face between my thighs, giving me a scrumptious lick.

I looped my hand behind his neck, and hoisting myself up, I draped both legs securely over his wide linebacker shoulders. His hands cupped my ass cheeks, lifting me midair, as he buried his face into my pulsating nether lips. His abrasive tongue lapped me like a starving beast. I panted, my hips arching. He growled, the vibrations pushing me to the edge. His long strokes had me writhing, my fingers clawing at his head.

"Not yet," he commanded, slowly rising from the chair, his head still buried in my center.

Effortlessly, he carried me over to the bed, dropping me with a bounce. He brushed a tender kiss across my lips and nuzzled my temple. I lay there as he stood and stripped out of his lounge pants. His golden skin was tight over the bulging muscles beneath. He was, without a doubt, the sexiest man I'd ever seen . . . and he was all mine.

My eyes dropped lower to his huge erection before he joined me on the bed. Sliding down my body, he pushed my leg out a little. Now I was even more exposed and vulnerable before his gaze.

He cupped my pussy. "This belongs to me."

In the blink of an eye, my legs were hooked over his shoulders. He settled himself between the V of my thighs. His tongue lapped me from my clit to the end of my cleft. He swirled his tongue around my clit, repeatedly flicking it, and then he sank it inside me. I panted, my hips arching. Holding me still, he unrelentingly fucked me with his wicked tongue. I hissed as he worked me into a frenzy, using sensual, long licks. His tongue constantly teased my opening.

"Who does this pussy belong to?" he gritted out as he pinned me.

I bucked as he continued to bathe me with his mouth.

"Whose is it, Hope?" He thrust two fingers into my trembling channel, curving them inside me, while pressing his thumb on my clit so his hand was clamped around me.

I was helplessly squirming and arching. "It's yours. Take all of me, Tiger," I responded breathlessly.

He made a low noise in his throat that pushed me to the edge of crazed lust. He shoved another finger inside me, making me cry out and buck.

My toes curled. I was so close. *Just one more swipe of his talented tongue . . .*

He raised his head, peering at me with sharpened eyes. My juices glistening on his lips like liquor filled me with perverse satisfaction and possessiveness.

I was greedy for more.

With one seamless motion, he withdrew his fingers, gripped my ass, and stabbed his tongue inside me. My back arched as I cried loudly for air to breathe. Consumed with lust, he continued relentlessly fucking me with his tongue.

My fingers reached down, biting into his silky hair, while he pumped me, drawing out my climax. Pulling my butt cheeks apart, he plunged one wet finger into the normally forbidden zone—my ass. My eyes rolled to the back of my head. I panted, drawing ragged breaths. Mercifully, he relented, pulling away, his eyes blazing with a focused animalistic wildness.

Holy hell.

I couldn't even form a coherent thought. Every muscle in my body tensed with expectation. I was so horny that all I wanted was to fuck.

"Fuck me," I demanded, all cavewoman-like.

He groaned before hauling me onto my knees. The cool air glided across the backs of my thighs. He ran a hand across the curve of my ass before parting my cheeks. A strange tingling sensation gripped my body like a vise.

"You're so damn sexy," he praised.

With sweet lust whipping through my dripping sex, I glanced over my shoulder, and I watched him reach into a large vase filled with condoms. He tore the package open with his teeth and quickly removed the latex.

In seconds, he sheathed his cock and curled his hand in my hair, snapping my head back. "Your pussy. Your ass. All of you. Mine," he whispered into my ear.

His grip on my hair tightened, and I moaned in response, the edge of pain taking me right where I needed to be.

Releasing my hair, he pressed me facedown onto the bed and buried himself so far inside me that my whole body quaked from the sheer force.

"Oh fuck!" I cried out as he ruthlessly stretched me.

He pushed forward, slow at first, and then he increased his speed from a sensuous slide to forceful pumping. "Fuck!" he cursed.

I couldn't move as Elijah rocked me, hard and steady. The feeling of helplessness ran through me, heightening every sensation in my body. He was driving me crazy with lust, and each stroke brought me closer and closer to the edge.

"Elijah," I groaned as he continued to fuck me like a man possessed.

The pressure tightened inside me before I brutally came

hard. I gasped and moaned as my interior muscles convulsed around him.

His fingers squeezed my hips. Again and again, he pulled out and plunged back inside me. He tensed, and every muscle rippled before he uttered a guttural groan that sounded like, "Mate," as his smooth pumping became jerky and harsh. He roared. His entire body shook as he came and came, his cock twitching inside me. He slumped over me, catching his weight on his hands. He nuzzled my neck and then pressed his sensuous mouth to the top of my shoulder before pulling gently out of me.

My breath became slow and easy.

"Let me take care of the condom." He disappeared for a second to dispose of it.

When he came back, tremors ran through me as his lips trailed across the back of my neck, causing my stomach to do flip-flops. Twisting me around, he enveloped me against his body by wrapping his arms around me. Effortlessly, he picked me up, cradling me. Pressing my head into the hollow of his shoulder, he carried me up to the head of the bed, as if I weighed nothing. When he tucked me against his body, I felt safe and comforted. Boneless, I curled against his chest while he pushed my damp strands of hair away from my forehead.

"I love you, Elijah," I whispered with drowsiness.

His hands clenched briefly and then released. "And I love you, Fae."

22

HOPE

I WOKE up the next morning, feeling sore everywhere. We'd had sex in almost every position imaginable, and then we'd ventured into some creative things I hadn't even known were possible. I was starving, but Elijah had warned me against eating anything in the fae realm because, according to folklore, I wouldn't be able to return to the human realm.

So I just took a shower before meeting the queen. After being escorted into an outdoor garden where Tianna was sitting and drinking what appeared to be coffee, I sat down next to her on the bench.

"Good morning, Hope. I have all of your stuff ready to go," she informed before her lips curled up into a sated smile that I recognized. It was the glazed stupor of being fucked . . . well.

"Risk?" I asked bluntly. "I'm guessing he wasn't opposed to . . . entertaining you?"

"Not at all," she drawled. "He seemed particularly agreeable to bondage and being tied to my bed. He's still there, laid out like a delectable morsel."

I wasn't sure if she was joking or not, but what happened in the bedroom stayed in the bedroom.

I stretched my legs. "Can I ask you a question about fae and sex?" I'd never felt more energetic in my life. The aura in the realm made me feel like I was riding a high that I hadn't come down from yet.

"Addicting, isn't it?" She laughed. "Fae use energy during sex, and we can also use sex to charge our spells. These are things you'll learn how to do over time. You'll have the power, if you keep having sex with Elijah, to open the portals for the demons. You just need to learn how to open portals on demand and make sure you are opening them up to the right realm. There are . . . spots in each realm where you can access portals to other realms. You just have to find them and learn how to read their energy signals."

"And I'm supposed to magically learn how to do this in, like, a day?" I asked, raising a brow. This was highly unlikely.

"Of course not, but that's why my seer will help you. You'll get there."

"I hope so," I grumbled. Then I realized there were other questions I needed to ask. "What about children? How does a fae's reproductive system work?"

"Like just about any other species . . . although we tend to have a harder time with getting pregnant. It's why we have so few children. It's why I don't have a child yet. I needed to find my mate in order to reproduce. As a female, it's rare for a non-mated fae to be able to have a child. Male fae can procreate with other species easier than our females. Females seem less receptive to conception when it's with a non-mated male. It's why Risk is tied to my bed."

"You weren't joking about him being tied to your bed," I mused aloud even though I'd meant to just think it. "Damn, that's freaky . . . in a spank-me-please way."

Tianna let out a laugh. The sound was musical and almost delicate. "There are so many things I want to do with him." She sighed with a happy glow on her face. "I've waited hundreds of years to find my mate. Risk is not going anywhere."

I wondered if Elijah would let me tie him up. I realized he

was more the type to tie me up, and then I pictured him tying me up.

Damn . . . that would be fucking hot.

Feeling my stomach tighten, I really needed to stop thinking about Elijah and sex. It was a distraction, and we had an entire lifetime to have sex. But that man had a gift for fucking. I wouldn't mind being tied up while he used his talented tongue to whip me into shape.

"When you saw the portal to our realm, what did it look like to you?" Tianna asked, snapping me out of my thoughts of Elijah tying me up, all cowboy-rodeo style.

"A ripple of water but in the air. Like crystal colors almost, it was sparkling but almost not there. It's hard to explain." I recalled the memory of the original portal and wasn't even sure how I'd walked through it. "It was just there, open to me. I put my hand through it, and when it disappeared, I walked in."

"Good. That's a start. A non-fae can't see the portal as a fae who has your bloodline can. You should be able to see any area that has the ability to access a portal. They'll be different colors, shapes, and sizes, based on the realm. Earth, for example, is gray to me rather than sparkly. It ripples and shimmers, but it looks more like clay than jewels. The demon realm has red and black, and the realm of angels is gold and misty."

"Wait, angels? As in, like, God?"

"Well, it depends on the god you refer to. Many gods have their own realms and their own angels. In this case, the realm I'm referring to is ruled by the goddess Aphrodite. She prefers her handmaidens to be called angels."

Tianna laughed when she saw the expression on my face. "Complicated, I know. I've had nearly a thousand years to master all this, and you're getting a crash course. You'll have time to become versed. You'll also need to learn to shield your powers as they manifest."

"What powers should I expect to get?"

"The beauty of being a fae is that our powers are unique to

each of us. When the time comes, you will know. Some fae have strong powers of speed, strength, clairvoyance, and the gift of transforming their appearance."

"Like a tiger-shifter?" I asked.

"No, my dear. Only your human appearance."

I blinked. "Wow."

She gestured to my hand. "May I touch you?"

I nodded.

Tianna caressed my hand. "I am seeing through your eyes that a demon was killed recently—no, two demons were killed by your tiger." Her lips curled up into a smile. "You are lucky. That tiger mate of yours is protective and strong." She moved her digits away from my hand.

My breath hitched. "So by touching an object or person, you can pick up their memories?"

"Yes. But that power is a blessing and a curse. Some memories can leave mental scars." She paused. "But like I said, your powers will come when the time is right. And the necklace your mother left you, wear it at all times. Not only is it a shield from other supernatural beings, but it will also help you charge your spells you'll want to use to control them better. You don't need it, but having a grounding agent will help you. From having too much energy, fae have been known to have unpredictable results at times with no way to control it."

"And I can talk to your seer?" I asked.

"Of course. Just use a mirror, and I'll give you a basic book of spells. You don't need to chant anything, but while you're learning, sometimes it helps to focus. And the spells sort of help guide the energy needed for the way you are trying to use it. In this case, since you don't use a crystal ball and aren't a witch and there aren't many other various ways, you'll need to use a mirror and your necklace to call upon the seer."

"Did you know my Uncle Frank? He mentioned something about being a guardian."

Tianna frowned. "His name is not familiar to me."

Tianna tilted her head and then gave a half smile. "You'll be escorted back to the portal. My mate is struggling against his bonds. I must attend to his needs before he hurts himself." She got up and glided away.

I took the opportunity to bask in the sun for a bit.

Then I went back to the suite I shared with Elijah, who was waiting for me. Walking over to him, I smacked a loud kiss across his cheek.

"Did you have a fun talk with the queen?" he asked.

"Yes, I think it's time to go home. We have a long road ahead of us, but I think I can at least deal with the demons now." I smiled, touching his cheek with my hand.

I quickly caught him up on our conversation before a knock interrupted us.

"Come in," I answered.

A man with dark hair and pale skin opened the door and stood there. "I'm here to guide you back to the portal for the human realm," he told us, his face showing no emotion.

"We're ready," I told him. I thought it was odd that the man never even acknowledged me.

When we got back to the portal, the man handed me a small sack. Inside were gems, a couple of scrolls, and a book. It also had a handheld silver mirror that looked like it would be worth a fortune back in the human realm.

The man handed Elijah a diminutive ornate gold box. "This is from the queen for the Harpy."

Elijah nodded. "I'll make sure she gets it."

After some false starts and a lot of swearing and cursing, I figured out how to pull the two of us through the portal. We stumbled to the other side, and I landed harder than I'd expected on the ground back in the forest.

"Damn, that's going to leave a nasty bruise," I grumbled.

Elijah extended his hand to me, pulling me up. "I'll make sure I run you a nice hot bath later." He kissed me on the lips. "Let's get the fuck out of here," he muttered as he held up his cell, trying to get a bar.

We had to walk a couple hours before Elijah finally got reception on his cell. First, he called Gina, giving her a long update, and then he called Twitch to come pick us up.

A COUPLE OF HOURS LATER, AFTER HIKING AWAY FROM THE portal, we met up with Twitch and Kraven at the appointed place and time. I was sitting in Elijah's vehicle with Kraven and Twitch trailing us in a black SUV. It was dark, and we were driving along a winding deserted road through the woods.

The music was playing, and the silence between us was comfortable as I stared out the window when, from a side road, a black vehicle slammed into the driver's door, sending us spinning around. My head cracked against the window. Dazed, I pressed a hand to my forehead. My fingers trembled when I felt the bleeding gash.

"Hope? You okay?" Elijah yelled.

My head was pounding as I tried not to give in to the wave of dizziness. "Yes. But we need—" My heart stopped when I saw two sets of crimson-red eyes coming toward the car.

Before Elijah could even open the door to get out, there were loud roars, growls, and screams, and then eerie silence.

The next thing I knew, a nude, blood-covered Twitch and Kraven were at our vehicle, prying the crushed metal open. My eyes widened at the sight of two bodies ripped apart, limb by limb.

"They were demons," Kraven growled.

❦ 23 ❧

ELIJAH

JUST THINKING about the audacity of the demons' attempt to kidnap Hope made my tiger roar. They could have killed her by slamming into my car, but that showed just how desperate and stupid the demons were. And it also proved they had no intention of giving up their quest to steal Hope.

After cleaning up the remnants of the demons the best we could, we left the scene. But I could tell Hope was shaken up from what had happened.

Hours later, Hope still had a pensive expression on her face as she stepped into my penthouse. So my number one priority was making her a relaxing hot bath with lots of aromatic bath salts and something hot and nourishing to eat.

Once I had my mate fed and rested, I tucked her against the couch. She seemed like she needed some quiet time to just think. So I gave her some space and went into my office to brief Gina via cell about the recent attempted attack by the demons. What had started out as a brief conversation turned into a long, troubling intel report from Gina.

According to Rogue intel, the Shadows predicament was worse than I'd originally thought. The Shadows were now spreading to other locations in the U.S. and targeting Others. In most cases, the demons were working right along with them.

My mind was still unraveling from the changing threat when I stormed into the living room. I was happy to see Hope was sitting on the couch with her feet curled under her and her fae book cradled in her lap.

"Did you talk to Harper?" I asked, dropping myself onto the couch next to her, sliding my feet onto the coffee table.

"Yes. She was catching a flight to meet up with Knox on his last leg of his tour. So I gave her the Cliff Notes on the whole fae and demon thing."

I shut my eyes, relaxing.

"Elijah?" Hope called, putting her hand on my thigh.

I quirked an eye open and peeked at her from under my lashes. "Uh-huh?" I asked her, feeling sleepy.

I hadn't had a good night's rest in a while. Between the nonstop need to take Hope in every freaky position possible and the whole demon debacle, I was exhausted.

"What are we going to do about the demons and Shadows?"

"Rogue intel says the situation with the demons and Shadows is getting worse. It's pretty much all hands on deck at Rogue. All resources are being reassigned to contain the brewing problem."

"And what about Declan?" Hope asked.

"Gina's trying to get in contact with him, but as usual, the fucker is being evasive," I growled. "But, on my end, I'm meeting up with Ryker and his pack this week to discuss how we can pool our resources together to annihilate the Shadows."

"I've been thinking about the Credence family, and I need to meet them. I think there's a connection between us that I need to explore."

"It's already in the works. And on another note . . ." I hesitated for a moment. "I'm not thrilled with this, but Gina wants to hire you."

She gasped. "She wants to give me a position as a Hunter?"

"Not exactly. More as a consultant to help with the demons and Shadows problem. With your unique abilities and many more that will be developing over time, she thinks you'll be a valuable asset to Rogue. You're tough, you can handle yourself, and you'll need a partner . . . me.

"You won't be doing any dangerous shit though." I shut my eyes for a moment before I cracked one eye open again, glimpsing at her shocked expression. "Unless, of course, you were thinking about something more low-key—you know, a white picket fence, a litter of cubs, and home-cooked meals every night. I like steak . . . medium rare."

"I don't do traditional anything, so get that shit out of your head, Tiger," Hope interjected with a laugh. "And I don't mind you occasionally cooking me a medium-rare steak." She saucily winked at me.

"I'll cook for my woman any day." I grinned at her.

"A job offer, huh?" She marveled while rubbing her chin. "I think I could handle that. And what about our living arrangement?"

"If you don't like my penthouse, I have a couple of houses, one Upstate and the other in Colorado," I remarked. "And if you don't want to live in either, just pick a place where you want to live, and we'll buy a house there. I'll give you the world, darling. I just want you to be happy."

"Okay, exactly how much does a Hunter make? With this penthouse and your two other homes, it doesn't equate."

"Not enough. I've invested well in several successful startups, including one owned by Cesar, that made me a millionaire. So financially, we're good," I responded. "We can live anywhere you want. We have Hunters all over the world. With modern-day technology, having an office in any location you pick wouldn't be impossible, and you'll need training and some small jobs before traveling would even be something that came up."

"So would Harpy keep your team together, or would she split you apart because of me?" She bit her bottom lip.

"No, the team will stay together. Not bragging, but we're her top Hunters. She needs us as a strong team. Occasionally, we travel to train newbie recruits, but that's it. It'll be okay, Hope, so stop worrying." I licked her bottom lip, dragging it between my teeth. I grabbed her face between my hands.

"Relax, Hope. We'll make this work. We can't pick apart every what-if scenario. Believe me; we'll figure this shit out." I softly kissed her lips. "No more talking."

My tongue entered her mouth as I straddled her on the couch. I pushed her into the back of the seat. She moaned against my lips, and when my hands started to wander, she grabbed my shoulders hard.

I let out a low growl. Damn, I liked when she was rough. It appealed to my cat nature, and it made me want to nibble on her and pin her down, feeling her squirm beneath me.

Kissing her more aggressively, I grabbed her wrists and held them above her head while I worked on nipping at her neck and shoulders. I let go and pulled on her shirt, popping the buttons, which flew everywhere.

Removing her bra in seconds, I buried my face against her ebony skin.

"And just for the record, I'd follow you to hell and back, Hope," I murmured before taking a nipple into my mouth and working my tongue around the little nub.

"Let us hope it doesn't come to that. Oh, right there. Don't stop," she told me. Digging her fingers into my scalp, tugging hard, she arched her back up, almost smothering me with her large breasts.

I switched to the other breast after a few minutes and let my hands go lower, working on the snaps on her pants. When I got them open, I stuck my hand under her panties, finding the swollen wetness showing she was almost ready for me.

I appreciated her sexuality and how much she loved intimacy. She was perfect for me, and I had no regrets—even if I ended up not doing as many missions or not putting myself in as much danger as I was used to. She was worth every minute of working more behind the scenes and on different assignments to keep her safe.

❧ 24 ❧

HOPE

ELIJAH SPRANG up from the couch. Instinctively, I wrapped my legs around his lean waist, digging my heels into his ass, as he effortlessly carried me through the penthouse, kicking his bedroom door open like he was the police.

Dropping me onto the bed, he straddled me, one knee on each side of my waist. I stared up at him with anticipation. His firm lips curved a little into a smile.

He stroked my hair. "Have you ever been tied?"

"No," I whispered. "I've never trusted anyone enough."

His eyes never left mine as he picked up my hands and lifted them toward the head of the bed, wrapping a soft strap around them. Excitement bubbled up in me as he moved to lie beside me.

He cupped my cheek in one huge hand, forcing me to meet his sensual gaze. "Do you trust me to take care of you?"

I nodded. He brushed a tender kiss across my lips and nuzzled my temple. I lay there, hands tied over my head, as he stood and slowly stripped. My eyes dropped lower as he slipped on a condom.

He knelt between my legs, hungrily eyeing me. He pushed

my leg out a little. He cupped my pussy. "Knees up to your stomach."

I blinked, bringing my knees up to my stomach. He pressed my knees outward, tipping my pussy up in the air.

He gazed straight into my eyes. "This is how I always want you—open and ready for whatever I want from you." He slid his fingers between the wet folds of my heat. "This pussy is mine to do with as I please."

I arched up, wiggling closer as he slipped his fingers inside.

His thumb circled and played with my clit. "Whether it is with my cock or mouth, this pussy is all mine."

I was dying for more even though I was on the edge of my first orgasm. As I stared at him, my mind grew numb. I needed more but was helpless. He stroked my heat, and I shivered. I was on the verge of exploding.

"Please," I whispered, "lick me."

His huge hands curled around my thighs, spreading me wider, and his tongue thrust into my heat. That one abrasive lick sent me spiraling over the edge, screaming his name like a prayer.

He pulled his head back and watched me as his fingers continued to stretch me. "Scream louder."

I was writhing and panting as my hips bucked wildly. His fingers thrust harder. I moaned louder when his finger found my clit again and mercilessly played with it. I screamed and came again, feeling lightheaded from the passion.

I must have blacked out because, by the time I caught my breath, Elijah was right above me, his weight on his knees between my thighs. He directed his condom-sheathed cock into position, smoothly slipping it in, eyeing me with burning possession.

He gave me a slow smile. "You are mine," he grunted, fully seated with his balls bumping against my ass.

He kissed my lips, my jaw, and my eyes. I basked in his tenderness and love. He pulled out and sank back in, hitting my

G-spot with precision. My legs wrapped around his waist. My pussy sucked him in farther as he pumped deeper. My hips tilted forward, and he adjusted his movements so with each stroke, he brushed deliciously against my clit. The deeper he pumped, the more I wanted him. My head snapped back as he slid in and out. I writhed beneath him, meeting him thrust for thrust. I was trembling, moaning low and deep.

He stilled my hips so I felt every inch of his pulsing cock.

"It's going to last all night," he growled in my ear as he released my arms from the bonds.

I slid my hands over his back, my nails digging into him like a wild woman. He continued pumping, hard and controlled.

I was going insane from the building heat. My breathing was fast and shallow with periods of whimpers intermixed.

"Please . . . harder." I grabbed his head, pulling him closer, biting his lower lip. "Please?"

He let himself go, moving faster, pushing me into another orgasm. Arching, I screamed as my pussy clenched around him. I collapsed right after, worn out and sweaty.

His face was harsh as he pulled from my body, flipping me onto my belly. He guided me up onto my knees. I moaned when he kissed my neck and shoulders and then rained kisses along my spine. He nudged me forward onto my hands. His growl was animalistic.

The air crackled around us as his strong hands gripped my waist, and his cock thrust into me. I cried out with pleasure as one hand gripped my hair while the other wrapped around my waist. His slick body rocked into me. Our bodies were in perfect synchrony, a strange magnetic energy wrapping around us.

"I'm yours . . . completely," I whispered, gripping the bed sheets.

He reared back and pushed forward. Every inch of him was sheathed in me. My body shook, my legs quivered, and my core pulsed, racing toward blissful release.

"Elijah . . ." I moaned.

"Hope Pippa, you're mine, and what I claim, I keep, cherish, love, and protect." His thrusts grew stronger as his body slapped against me.

My fingers clenched the sheets as I rocked back into his body. My body burned for sweet release. A strangled shout escaped his lips before he bit the spot between my neck and shoulder. I came so hard I screamed his name at the top of my lungs.

My inner muscles contracted, milking him. He roared, his rigid shaft pulsing deep into my scorching core, both of us cresting. He kissed me on my shoulder before pulling me up farther onto the bed. Clutching me against his body, he kissed me, and with eyes closed, I kissed him back.

With every fiber in my body, I knew this man would love me hard and treasure me until his last breath.

I moaned with content as we held on to each other, our lips melding over and over as the tremors passed.

He nuzzled my neck. "I waited an eternity for you, and I'm never letting you go," he drawled, nibbling on my ear.

He found the mark he'd left on my shoulder and gently licked it. A strange tingling sensation rippled my body.

I exhaled heavily, cuddling into his body. "I love you, Elijah Beastie."

His mouth trailed to my neck, biting over his mark of possession. "I'll love you 'til the day I die, Hope Pippa." He wrapped his arms around my waist and squeezed.

We started to doze off when his cell phone rang. He answered it and listened without saying a word to the other person talking. His jaw tightened. When his call ended, I waited for him to tell me what was going on.

"Well, it appears our new job starts today. We have a rogue vampire in the area who's been turning people without sticking around and teaching them how to be a vampire, and it's caused a couple of his turns to kill people, since they didn't know how to feed without . . . Well, you get the idea. Our job is to round up all his turns, locate the vampire turning them, and bring him in for questioning," Elijah told me before pulling me up and effortlessly draping me over his shoulder. "The team is preparing and gathering info, so we have time for a shower."

"You really have to stop this caveman shit. I can walk," I grumbled.

He just laughed and slapped my ass, striding into the bathroom and plopping me onto the granite vanity. He took off the condom, cleaned himself up, and sheathed his straining erection with a new condom.

I eyed him. "I'm assuming bathing isn't the only thing you plan on doing."

"I hope not," Elijah told me as we got into the shower together.

"Now it's time for your big, bad tiger to show you how much I need you . . . again." His mouth crushed onto mine as his tongue thrust forcefully into my mouth, sweeping against mine. He nipped me hard on my chin as he raised my leg, pulling it over his muscular ass, before sinking his cock into me.

I shivered deliciously as he sank his teeth into my neck. "Elijah." I gasped, digging my nails into his shoulders, as the orgasm gripped me.

He growled, "Mine." His nose pressed against my neck as he breathed in my scent. "So you really have tamed the Beastie."

I touched his cheek. "Absolutely."

Thank you for reading **TAMING THE BEAST!**

More Credence Curse Series goodness continues with **REASON TO LOVE!**

Vampire princesses can't be tamed... unless it's by a dominant Alpha desperate to make her his mate.

GET A FREE SEDONA VENEZ BOOK!

https://sedonavenez.com/free-book

WANT FREE SEDONA VENEZ BOOKS?

Sign up for Sedona Venez's Newsletter and receive FREE BOOKS. In addition to the free stories, you will also get special pricing, exclusive previews and news of new releases.

GET A FREE SEDONA VENEZ BOOK!

Join Sedona's mailing list to be the first to know of new releases, free books, special prices and other author giveaways.

https://sedonavenez.com/free-book

OTHER TITLES BY SEDONA VENEZ

SciFi Romance
Galaxy Alien Warriors - The Box Set
Beauty and the Alien Beast

Paranormal Romance
Shifter Alphas Furever Series
Claimed by Her Two Alphas
Claimed by Her Wolf
Claimed by Her Bear
Claimed by Her Dragon

Paranormal Romance
Credence Curse Series
When Lightning Strikes
Taming the Beast
Reason to Love

Wolf Shifter Romance
Wolf Elite Series
Operation Wolf: Gunner
Operation Wolf: Eli

Operation Wolf: Hunter

Bears Shifter Romance
Bear Elite Series
Bear's Mission

Enemies-to-Lovers Romance
Dirty Secrets Series
Twisted Lies
Twisted Lies 2
Twisted Lies 3
Twisted Lies 4

Friends-to-Lovers Romance
Heart of Fire

MFM Ménage Romance
Standalone
Shameless Desires

Billionaire Boss Romance
Standalone
Mr. Billionaire CEO

Urban Fantasy Romance
Magic Fire Collection

ABOUT THE AUTHOR

USA TODAY BESTSELLING AUTHOR SEDONA VENEZ lives in New York City with her hot ex-military hubby—hooah—and their fur babies. She loves writing sizzling, sexy intricate stories about strong but broken characters who push limits, overcome their fears and risk it all for love.

Sedona loves to connect with readers!
www.sedonavenez.com